THE BALLAD OF EDISON BESTWELL

Best Wishes

Jason Keller

THE *Ballad* OF EDISON BESTWELL

BY JASON KELLER

iUniverse, Inc.
Bloomington

THE BALLAD OF EDISON BESTWELL

iUniverse books may be ordered through booksellers or by contacting:

iUniverse
1663 Liberty Drive
Bloomington, IN 47403
www.iuniverse.com
1-800-Authors (1-800-288-4677)

ISBN: 978-1-4759-8832-1 (sc)
ISBN: 978-1-4759-8831-4 (hc)
ISBN: 978-1-4759-8830-7 (e)

Library of Congress Control Number: 2013907658

Printed in the United States of America

iUniverse rev. date: 5/24/2013

For my parents, Jeff and Peggy

"The world is indubitably one if you look at it in one way, but as indubitably is it many, if you look at it in another."—William James

Acknowledgments

My deepest gratitude goes out to my family, including my parents, Jeff and Peggy, and my brothers, Justin, Josh, Jake, Drew, and Isaiah. I would also like to thank the Chatfield clan, especially my aunt Deb, whose encouraging words and feedback were crucial to this story. I am grateful to my grandmothers, Betty and Susie, who taught me more than they could ever imagine, and to all the friends who grew up with me, for enriching my life and providing the memories that influenced this book. A special thanks to Barry Blevins—or should I say Ben—my oldest and best friend. To Harris Lenowitz, thank you for teaching me more about language usage than anybody else on the planet. And to the editorial department at iUniverse, especially Krista, Claire, and Stephanie, thank you; this story would not be what it is without your assistance. And most of all, I am grateful to my savior, Jesus Christ, who provides the way for us all.

I

MY NAME IS EDISON BESTWELL. Everybody calls me Eddie, though. Hardly anybody even knows that my name is really Edison. I think my mother named me that in hopes that I would be a genius or something, like someone naming their kid Jordan in hopes that he'll be able to play basketball, or Mariah in the expectation that she'll be able to hit a high note. I may not be a savant, but don't let the fact that I'm a backwoods hillbilly fool you either—I've seen a few things in my time. I was born in 1969 in Cripple Creek, Kentucky, a town nestled in the foothills of the Appalachian Mountains, where generations of hill people carved their way through the area just like the rivers and streams that shaped the land. Times were simpler when I was a child, and people seemed happy to just saunter along the path of life without much fuss. The Shawnee Indians roamed these hills first, with their natural religion to guide them. A great Shawnee chief is said to have roamed this region too. At the moment of his birth, his father, Pucksinwah, saw a meteor streak across the sky, and he named his son Tecumseh, which means "the panther passing across." That story stuck with me as my best friend Ben Baldridge and I wandered the surrounding country as kids. Ben's older sister, Lilly, would tag along most of the time as well. She was two years older than us, but she was the runt of the family, and if you were to line us all up together, you would've thought we were all born in the same litter. Ben and Lilly's resemblance was remarkable except that Ben had the haircut of an enlisted soldier, whereas Lilly's flaxen locks flowed abundantly past her shoulders. It seems like the first thing I remember about life is these hills and the people that belong to them.

When Ben and I entered third grade, Mrs. Bender sat us all in rows, in alphabetical order, like this was supposed to instill some sense of order to the Chinese fire drill that was her classroom. That placed me right behind Ben in the middle of row one. And as fate would have it, the apple of my eye, Cristina Jenkins, sat directly next to me in row two. I don't know if there is an official age one has to reach to legitimately fall in love, but I guess I hit my stride early. When I first saw that girl, it felt like a donkey kick to the chest. But you know how young'uns are—it would take me the better part of that school year to muster up the nerve to talk to her, and when I did, I nearly peed my pants.

But Ben and I were inseparable. We would chum around the schoolyard talking about how we were gonna be oceanographers one day. I don't even know where we got that crazy idea, but it sure did stick. We would dig through encyclopedias, finding every fact and picture about every fish we could. And we had these notebooks with all these sketches of fishes, with facts neatly listed beside them, page after page. We would talk for hours about adventures on the high seas, searching for the answers to the mysteries hidden in the deep.

Little did we know that a whopper of a mystery was in our future. The things we saw implicated us, and our curious minds involved us, so as luck would have it, we were entangled from the get-go. The mystique would soon grow into something that we never could have imagined.

But we'll get to that soon enough. As I was saying, Ben and I were like peas and carrots, thick as thieves, and I started riding the school bus home with him so we could continue planning all the adventures we had in mind. Ben lived up the hollow just like nearly everybody else in Cripple Creek. Growing up in

Appalachia had its ups and downs. Everybody I knew was dirt poor, including Ben's family. But they were good people. Ben's mom, Nell, worked in the cafeteria at school and always knew what kind of trouble Ben and I were up to. The trouble was innocent enough, though, stuff like skipping class to go fishing down at the river or turning a snake loose in Mrs. Bender's desk drawer. And she was always bringing leftovers home from the cafeteria, which meant chili and peanut butter sandwiches three or four nights a week.

We were always in the woods. We knew every game trail and creek bed like the back of our hand. The hills became a part of who we were. I can see how the natives and settlers felt drawn to it, like the land was adopting them. That's the way us hill folks are. The land doesn't belong to us; we belong to the land.

But walking back toward Ben's house on the road from the end of the hollow always gave us the creeps—a real bona fide case of the heebie-jeebies. This always happened because we had to walk past the old run-down barn that sat on the edge of the Baldridges' property, a half a mile or so down the road from their house, where the road turned from pavement to dirt. The township never saw fit to pave the whole road, I guess, 'cause only the Hayfields lived up at the end of the hollow, and they hardly went anywhere except for when Mrs. Hayfield delivered her homemade pies to DeeDee's Diner. Such a thing wasn't so rare in Cripple Creek—everything 'round these parts ran on a shoestring budget. Most everybody was pretty much self-sufficient. Just about everyone I knew grew their own crops to feed themselves and kept some cattle and pigs around to slaughter for meat. It's not like there was much to go to town for anyway. All we had were a couple of diners and dollar stores and the Family Fuel-Mart where you could get your gas and groceries all at the same place. It was pretty big news when Cripple Creek got its second red light out where the highway runs through. Oh yeah, and there was the drive-in movie screen out off Route 60 near Owensville where the movies became alive with the backdrop of the hills. It was a magical place.

But that barn had to be the creepiest place in the world as far as I was concerned. It looked like it was about a hundred years old and nearly ready to fall in on itself. It looked as if you could kick one of the boards that had turned sickly gray with age, and the whole thing would just come crumbling down and turn into dust. And it just smelled *stale* around the area where it stood, like the place was sick or something.

Ben and I would be walking down the road with not a care in the world, and as soon as we got near that barn, our pace and our pulse would quicken with equal intensity until we were galloping on past as fast as our legs could carry us. We wouldn't slow down until we were well past and looking over our shoulders—just to make sure, ya know. Man, that place sure did give us the willies.

I guess we kind of always just *knew*, ya know. I think kids are more sensitive to evil. The closer they are to the innocence of infancy, the more keenly attuned their senses are to corruption. And when I say evil and corruption, I mean ... well, I'm getting ahead of myself again.

The summer between our fifth- and sixth-grade years was one of those magical summers of childhood, the ones where it seems like you make a lifetime of memories in one season. Ben and I were always together. My house was two or three miles away by car, but if you went over the hill right behind Ben's place and through the woods a ways, you would come out right into my backyard. We would meet halfway, where the hill came down to meet the creek that ran all the way to the river. Cristina was with us a good bit of the time as well. Since I'd broken the ice with her back in third grade, we kinda took a liking to one another, and we were now an item. She would go fishing with us down at the river, and she would even bait her own hook. Cristina was growing up to be quite the looker with her long dark hair and eyes to match. She looked like she

4

could be a little model or something. But you couldn't let that fool you—she could hunt and fish better than most boys our age. That summer was full of memories. It was the summer that Cristina and I first kissed.

It was also the summer that Lilly went missing.

2

I REMEMBER THAT DAY LIKE IT was yesterday. It seems that when something big happens, whether it's good or bad, it gets seared into your memory for time and all eternity.

It also happened to be during one of the worst storms that Cripple Creek had seen in years. Trees were laid over everywhere, and the town was without power for over twenty-four hours. They said that up to five tornados were spotted in Johnson County. It seems the storm was a harbinger of things to come.

The day before, Ben and I were outside behind his house ranging about the toolshed when Ben's mom came out and told me I'd better be making tracks for home. The radio was sending out severe weather warnings for all of Johnson County. It had been sprinkling earlier, but there was an eerie calm presiding when I started off for home. I went the usual route over the hill, and I was about halfway when it hit. The storm descended on the forest like an eagle on its prey. Wind gusts were soon knocking me sideways. The trees groaned against the storm, and with the cracking of broken limbs, it soon became a symphony of devastation. I kept moving, and I was never more glad to reach home.

***

The next morning I came shuffling into the kitchen in my pajamas. "Eddie, when was the last time you saw Lilly?" my mom asked as I pulled on the handle of the fridge.

7

"I don't know. I took off for home before the storm hit," I said as I grabbed the pitcher of orange juice.

Before I could turn around, my mom grabbed me by the shoulders and gave me a little shake. "Eddie"—I immediately sensed the panic in her voice—"never mind the orange juice. This is important. When was the last time you saw Lilly?"

"Over at Ben's, I guess. Why?" I was confused, and I could see that my mom was frazzled. Her long brown hair had not received its obligatory brushing, and the skin around her eyes was swollen and red.

"Well, Lilly is missing, and they're over there looking everywhere for her, and your daddy went to see if he could help." She grabbed me and pulled me in toward her. I could feel her shaking. I thought of Ben.

"Do you think she got caught out in the storm?" I asked.

"I don't know."

"Is Sheriff Jenkins over there?" I asked, now alarmed.

"Half the county's over there looking for her, sweetie!" my mom snapped. And right then I fully realized what was going on. Panic flowed over me like a wave of nausea. I imagined what it must be like over there, with the lights on the sheriff's car lighting up the hollow and the men slogging up the hills in the early morning fog, calling Lilly's name over and over. Where was Ben in all of that? Was he out in front with a light, hollering her name, or was he just sitting wide-eyed back at his house with no idea what was going on, just like me right here? I felt a knot in the pit of my stomach.

***

They had realized she was missing the previous day, right before the storm hit. Bulletins had been broadcast on radio and television for severe weather, and everyone was preparing to batten down the hatches. Earlier, she had ridden her bike into town to buy some thread for her mom but hadn't returned. Earl and Nell drove to the dollar store where she was supposed to go, but there was no sign of her. Nell ran inside and asked the cashier if she'd seen Lilly. The answer was no.

When the wind started picking up, Nell became frantic. She tried calling everywhere she could think of, but some telephone lines had already been knocked out, making it impossible to track Lilly down. Earl calmed his wife down a little by telling her she had probably gone to the nearest safe place when the weather bulletin went out. Eventually the storm started raging through the hollow, and everybody had to hunker down and wait it out. Later that evening, when things had somewhat subsided, they went out to start looking for her. All telephone service was out, so they took off in the truck, but there were trees and power lines down everywhere making the search difficult. No matter, the search had begun.

***

Things were a bit tense around Cripple Creek during the days and weeks following Lilly's disappearance. Speculation and conjecture ran rampant in town. Nothing this scandalous had happened in Johnson County since Pete Giles shot his uncle over a bologna sandwich back in '74. (A bologna sandwich, can you imagine that?) But this time, it was more than a bologna sandwich. After the sheriff's office turned up a big pile of jack squat, the FBI came down from the Lexington office to officially register Lilly as a missing person and to do their own little investigation. They turned up the same thing that the sheriff's office had: jack squat. And then it was case closed. You gotta understand that this was in backwoods Kentucky in 1979. The resources simply did not exist. Besides, it was like she'd just up and vanished. Poof. Gone.

3

Cripple Creek Kentucky, 1987

BEN AND I LOST OUR dreams of being oceanographers like the sea captain loses his view of home to the horizon. It just drifted away. But we were tight as a pine knot, and life in Cripple Creek was back to normal, whatever that was. Nobody ever mentioned Lilly; it was like she'd never existed. After all, seven years had passed, and time is the balm that fades the remembrance of tragedy. But it was always in the back of my mind. And yep, Cristina and I were still an item, except for now we had both gone through puberty. But we survived it without any major incidents, if ya know what I mean. Besides, Cristina's dad also happened to be the sheriff, so if he said, "Have her home by ten o'clock," I'd have her home by a quarter till.

I'd been driving all sorts of machinery around the farm since I was seven years old, but when I became legal to drive, I thought I was as smooth as the cat's behind. I am two months older than Ben to the day, so I got my license to drive before he did. When I turned seventeen, my dad saw fit to buy me a 1966 Mustang, and I fully embraced the notion of burning rubber. It felt like I'd been waiting my whole life to take Cristina to the drive-in in my own car. But I can tell you the sheriff wasn't too game on that idea. On the nights that we went there, the sheriff's car must've driven in and out of that place twenty times.

We fell in love with booze. In this part of Kentucky, we

didn't have to travel all the way to Owensville to buy whiskey at the state liquor store. We brewed our own corn liquor—moonshine—and it was good. But the first time Sheriff Jenkins caught a whiff of that stuff on my breath after I brought Cristina home, that was it. She was forbidden to even whisper my name. We both took it pretty hard, but we figured it would eventually blow over. Besides, we'd sneak and see each other from time to time anyway.

That's when me and Ben got back to the business of fishin'. Countless were the nights that we would sit on the riverbank fishing for catfish and drinking shine till early in the morning. The fog would roll in so thick in the middle of the night that you couldn't see the river. We'd put bells on our fishing poles so we would know when we were getting a bite because sometimes you couldn't even see the end of your pole.

That's the kind of night it was when this little situation of ours took on a whole different perspective.

We were camping in the hills behind Ben's house. There were four of us: me, Ben, Tommy Lang, and Rodney Stillwater. Tommy's people lived over on Blue Run, so Tommy was always riding his Kawasaki dirt bike over to Ben's place to meet up with us, and Rodney found his way to wherever we were by his own stealthy ways. Problem with that is, Rodney would show up armed to the teeth like he was startin' an insurrection or something. He loved his guns and fully participated in his right to bear 'em. If there were any of us young'uns, besides Ben, of course, who seemed deeply troubled by Lilly's disappearance, it was him. Ever since that fateful day, a subtle anxiety clung to him like a wet shirt. Rodney was a bit off too, if you know what I mean. I don't want to say that he was crazy 'cause I don't think it would have mattered anyway—with what happened, I mean.

Our campsite was one of our usual haunts. It sat in a clearing just below the ridgeline that faced Ben's place, where we could barely make out the lights coming from his house. I do believe it was one of the most peaceful spots on earth, but not on this night. The moonshine flowed heavily, and we were smokin' a bit of that backwoods herb too. The usual shenanigans ensued.

The dancing and singing died out about midnight, and things seemed to be coming to their end. I was dozing off sitting next to Ben, who was passed out. He'd been going on and on about some tart that he'd met at the drive-in. "Built like a burlap sack full of bobcats," I believe is how he put it. Now he was just a slobbering mess, but nonetheless a peaceful silence dominated the night, broken only by the crackle of the campfire that drifted through the trees. Tommy was kicked back with his hands neatly folded across his belly, and he looked as content as a baby. And then ... *bang!*

The pop of the gunfire brought us all up to our feet and somewhat to our senses. Rodney. Hot Rod. The nickname suited him. That jackrabbit son of a gun was wound tighter than a drum and about as predictable as a striped snake, and he had just scared us boys right back into reality. I instinctively scurried behind the nearest tree, trepidation shooting through me like crap through a goose. Tommy soon joined me.

"What the ..." Ben shouted as he staggered about, trying to find his hat.

Tommy looked at me with eyes as wide as dinner plates as we all looked around for Rodney, but the pitch-black night was made heavier by the fog, and we couldn't see five feet in front of our faces. All we had was this little bubble that the fire had burned out for us, and Rodney wasn't in it.

"I'm coming, Lilly!" we heard Rodney shout, and we knew from the sounds of breaking branches and crumpling leaves that he was moving quickly through the forest.

Ben jerked his head around like the snap of a whip. The atmosphere of confusion was now amplified by what Rodney had just roared out. *Lilly?* I thought to myself. What was Rodney thinking, hollering her name? I knew Ben had to be thinking the same thing.

"What the heck is he doin', Eddie?" Tommy whispered, and Ben gave a quick "shh" with his finger to his lips. Earlier I had observed Rodney taking notably large swills from his dad's homemade whiskey that he'd brought with him. He was high on shine and obviously out of his mind, and we were trying to figure out where he was lurking. Tommy and I slowly emerged from behind the tree.

"Rodney, you stupid hilljack, where are you?" I shouted. I was used to a certain amount of this kind of thing, but something about what was happening right in front of me was out of place and out of time. I was scared.

"Quit your messin' around, Rodney!" Tommy shouted, which got another shush from Ben.

Ben and I made eye contact, and we didn't have to speak. We both knew that something really bad was going down.

We heard Rodney moving away from us and down the hill. We all looked around at each other with the same thought in our minds: *What do we do now?*

"We better get after him," Ben said as he pulled his jacket over his shoulders.

"Just what do you mean, we better get after him?" Tommy protested, fear in his eyes. He seemed just fine with staying put.

"Are you okay, Ben?" I asked. I knew that the mere mention of Lilly's name usually upset Ben, so I figured he had to be pretty shaken.

"Yeah." He stared into the fog-shrouded night. "I reckon we better try to round him up."

I looked over at Tommy, who was visibly upset. "You can stay here, Tommy, but Ben and I are going after Rod."

"If you think that I'm gonna stay here alone, you're off your rocker," Tommy said as he hastily started lacing up his boots.

"Okay then," I heard Ben say from somewhere in front of me. I took a deep breath and stepped into the night behind him.

* * *

It wasn't too hard to follow after Rodney. It was autumn, and most of the leaves had already fallen off the trees, so you couldn't walk anywhere through the hills without making a racket. But that meant Rod could hear us following him too, if that even mattered.

"Rod, where ya going, man? It's us—Eddie, Ben, and Tommy!" I shouted, knowing that I sounded corny and a bit pretentious. Rodney didn't answer. We listened to him dash down the hill, and we gave pursuit. On a clear, moonlit night, the odds of us chasing him down would've been in our favor, but the soupy thick fog made it an entirely different ball game. Paths, game trails, and points of reference were cloaked in the chilly, condensed moisture of the air. We ran with our hands reached out before us to deflect the branches and limbs that appeared out of nowhere in the mist. Brush and fallen timber tripped our feet and grabbed at our legs as we stumbled through the forest. "Where are we?" Tommy asked with labored breath as we lumbered through the darkness.

"Not sure. This fog is so thick, I can't get my bearings," I replied.

And just then, *bang!* Another shot from Rodney's pistol. It was a Dan Wesson 357, I believe. He'd showed it off to us earlier in the night. "My handheld cannon," he'd said.

"*Lilly!*" we heard Rodney shout after the explosion of the pistol echoed across the hollow. Again I knew how poignant this must have felt to Ben because it aroused deep emotions even within me.

"Rodney, you stop this right now! Stop shootin' off that pistol!" Tommy yelled.

We found ourselves on a steep slope sliding down through the wet leaves and branches. I tried to remember being at this spot before, but I couldn't get myself oriented with the fog so thick and the adrenaline running like a river through my veins.

Soon we heard the splashing of water—the creek. We were at the bottom of the hill. The fog had settled thicker here in the valley, making it nearly impossible to figure out just where in hell's half-acre we were. We came to a stop in the ankle-deep water.

We heard Rod run through the creek, and then the noise of his movement stopped. We looked at each other with deer-in-headlights expressions.

"Where are we, Eddie?" Tommy asked.

"We're off the hill—that's about all I know."

We crossed the creek and found ourselves on flat ground. There were no trees.

"I think we're in a field," said Ben.

"Yeah, but which field?" I replied.

No wonder we couldn't hear ole Hot Rod anymore. For all we knew, he could've taken off in any direction. Then we heard him.

"*Lilly!*"

"That way," Ben said, pointing in the direction of the shout.

We all grabbed ahold of each other and took off across the field. Our pant legs were soaking wet from wading through the water. We could feel the fog parting as we knifed our way toward Rodney. I felt it move through my lungs as we lurched across the field. It had become a beast. We pressed on. Then we hit a wall, literally.

"What the ..." I said as I put my hand against the boards that blocked our way. I stepped sideways, keeping my hands on the vertical slabs of wood. As I continued across the boards, my hand burst through a small opening. Startled, I withdrew my hand and felt the sill of a large window as the smell of wet, rotting hay permeated my nostrils. Suddenly, my heart dropped low in my chest. I knew exactly where we were.

16

"Ben, we're at the barn, man!" I snapped. I couldn't believe it—I didn't think we were anywhere near it—but there it stood, right in front of us, big as you please.

"Yeah, this is not good," said Tommy, but Ben was just staring at the sickly gray boards, not saying a word.

"Ben," I muttered quietly as I put my hand on his shoulder. "What's going on, brother?"

"This place," Ben said as he reached out and touched the barn. "Why this place, Eddie?"

"I don't know, man. I don't know what's got into him," I said. I slung my arm around his back with sympathy.

"*Rodney!*" Tommy shouted.

We heard a whimper coming from inside the barn. That got our attention really fast.

"Shh." I put my fingers to my lips. "Listen."

We crept closer to the barn, pressing our ears to the boards. We could hear Rodney mumbling and sobbing somewhere inside the dreaded place.

"What now, Eddie?" Tommy asked.

"I don't know, man. This place really gives me the creeps!" I could feel a heavy sense of dread slinking around the barn, like the devil himself had brought down this fog onto us and shrouded our lives within this moment. We shrank with the weight of what was happening, huddled together outside the barn.

Then it was just us breathing. Silence. Nothing.

A moment later, the explosion from the gun blast lit up the barn for a millisecond as light burst forth from every crack between the stale boards. We fell back as if we'd been hit with a jackhammer. Then darkness descended again, and a heavy silence fell.

***

We just stood there looking at the barn. I could smell the gunpowder from the blast. I had a feeling of intense dread, like I was about to start a walk to the gallows. But it wasn't the gallows—it was that dreaded barn, and I knew I had to go inside. All the days spent around these hills, and I'd never been inside that barn. Never. And neither had Ben. It had been an unspoken thing for as long as either of us could remember. Now here we stood, as big as you please, knowing we had to go inside.

"Rodney?" Ben said, breaking the silence.

"This is gonna end right here, Rodney. You hear me?" I yelled.

But there was no response.

I crept closer to the barn, moving toward the door. "You hearing me, Rodney?" I crept closer still, reaching through the fog to the handle on the door. I grasped it, threw the latch board up, and pulled on the door. It made a sickly sound as it opened.

I stepped inside the barn and immediately sensed that things had taken a turn toward terrible. There was an oppressive air in the place. Inside the air was heavier. Colder.

"Get out your lighter, Ben," I said. The darkness took on a different perspective inside the barn. It was more acute. It became a presence that was enclosing us, yoking us with the weight of fear.

Ben fumbled for his lighter and finally got it lit, revealing the interior of the barn. Everything was cast in the warm yellow-orange glow as Ben held the lighter above his head. We looked toward the other end of the barn, but the revealing light from the flame invaded the barn's darkness only about halfway, to where the horse stables began.

For the first time I felt as if something else was present, something besides us, something different from us. Quickly, I glanced at Ben and Tommy. Even in the dim light, I could see a nervous tick twitching in Ben's cheek. Tommy was clenching and unclenching his fists. I could tell that they felt it too.

"Rodney!" I shouted.

There was still no answer.

I turned back and looked at Ben and Tommy, seeking an encouraging word or gesture. Ben finally nodded as if to say, "Well, go on." I motioned for them to follow so that I could see out in front of the halo created by the lighter. As we inched closer to the back of the barn, a knot was burgeoning in the pit of my stomach. I could sense the unease of the place. Running past the barn years earlier as a child, I'd had the same creepy feeling that I felt now. And there was the smell. Gunpowder and fresh-cut meat: that's what it smelled like.

Just as we were passing the first stall, I heard a voice, a female voice, very low and soft. The sound floated past me and through me like a wisp. I stumbled backward a couple of steps and ran into Tommy. "I heard a voice," I said in a loud whisper. "Did you hear it?"

"I didn't hear nothin', man."

"Me neither."

"Shh!"

"Well, I think I just heard a girl's voice over there," I said as I pointed to the back left corner of darkness. As I looked past my finger to where I was pointing, I realized that my whole arm was trembling. I quickly pulled it down to my side, took a deep breath, and started toward the back of the barn. I had to find out what was happening. I walked toward the stall directly in front of me with Ben and Tommy following a few steps behind. As I inched closer, I felt as if something was pulling me toward the stall. I came close enough to grab the handle on the stall door and reached slowly toward it. Breathing heavily and slowly, I pulled on the latch and let the door come creaking open.

Rodney was slumped on the ground like a drunk taking a nap. But on the one side of his head that we could see, there was a gaping exit wound in front of and a little higher than his ear. Shards of Rod's skull were protruding through the skin, revealing brains and blood. His right hand still held the .357 that he had been bragging about earlier. Behind me I heard

Tommy turn and throw up. I brought my hands up to cover my mouth and whispered, "Oh no." Rodney Stillwater had shot himself.

Why? Why would he do this? My thoughts scrambled in my mind. I knew he was wired tight and a bit impish, but this ... this was something entirely different. And why had he been shouting Lilly's name? I was overwhelmed by the tumult of emotion and tension.

***

"What do we do now?" Ben screamed as he paced back and forth in the barn. He let the lighter go out, and the darkness was intense. I couldn't move; I was in a state of shock. And Tommy had been reduced to a whimpering mess. I was trying to think, but I couldn't. Even in the darkness, all I could see was Rodney's brains oozing out of the wound in his head.

Then we heard her. At first it was just an apprehensive sobbing, but then we heard her speak. "H-h-help ... me."

Ben flicked his lighter back on, and the center of the barn became alive again in the glow of the flame. The voice had come from another stall in the barn. We all looked at each other, as if to see whether we were indeed all hearing the same thing. We stared at each other in silence for a moment, waiting, fearing. Tommy swallowed hard and wiped the vomit from his mouth. We all looked in the direction of the voice just as it arose again. "Help me, p-p-please."

As if compelled by some unseen force, we moved slowly and all at once toward the voice. The stall door was slightly ajar, as if to invite us to peer inside. Ben lifted the lighter a bit higher, casting an ever-so-slight glow inside the stall. I reached out and nudged the door open and then jumped back, expecting something to leap out at me. Moments earlier when we'd found Rodney in the other stall, I thought I'd had the shock of a lifetime, but I was even less prepared to see what was before me now.

There in the stall was Lilly. Shivering and with eyes as scared as any I'd ever seen, she peered at us over her knees, which were pulled up to her chest. She looked at me as if she didn't know me—it had been seven years. But there was something else. She looked the same. In the shock of seeing her, I hadn't immediately realized that I was looking at the same twelve-year-old girl who had disappeared so long ago; she hadn't aged. How could that be?

4

DEPUTY JIMMY ALLEN SAT IN the Johnson County sheriff's office ogling Miss July. Rifling through back issues of *Playboy* was a common practice on a late Friday night at the front desk where Jimmy sat. He leaned back in the padded seat with his skinny legs propped up on the pile of folders beside the telephone. The office was as quiet as an empty box, as was the town. On late weekend nights, people looking for entertainment were either out at the drive-in or up the hollow, gathered at each other's places, drinking sarsaparillas and playing music. The radios couldn't pick up much more than news and weather, so if people wanted music, they had to make their own. The sounds of banjos and guitars were as natural as the harmony of crickets and frogs that permeated the hills.

Earlier Jimmy had dispatched fellow deputy John Quills to investigate an unwanted presence in Miss Clary Stewart's garage, which turned out to be a raccoon. Jimmy had rolled his eyes when Deputy Quills radioed back to report that the situation was under control. "At least we can all relax now," Jimmy said aloud to himself in the empty office. Together Jimmy Allen and John Quills represented the law of the land on this particular Friday evening in Cripple Creek. A normal middle of Friday night at the Johnson County sheriff's office meant pie from Mrs. Hayfield's kitchen—peach custard, cherry, banana cream, blueberry, blackberry, or, of course, apple. Pies were brought in as fresh as it gets around 4:30 a.m. She delivered her homemade goodness every Saturday and Sunday to DeeDee's Diner, which sat right across the street from the municipal building on Main Street. Mrs. Hayfield always made an extra pie or two for the deputies. You have to grease the wheel, ya know. She never missed a delivery on that late Friday/early Saturday for nearly thirty years. Blizzards, floods, holidays, funerals, births, deaths, fires—nothing could stop her from doing her duty.

When the phone rang at exactly 4:39 a.m., Jimmy had his feet propped up on the corner of the desk with the magazine splayed across his lap, his mouth full of warm apple pie. As he sat up to answer the phone, he made quick work of the pie and wiped his mouth. He picked up the telephone.

"Sheriff's office."

On the other end of the line was the frantic voice of Nell Baldridge. Jimmy's eyes went wide as he listened, and he abruptly jumped to his feet.

***

When the sheriff raised his head to look at the alarm clock, the oppressive glare of the red LEDs read 4:45. As he rubbed his eyes, the phone rang for the third time. Harlen Jenkins sat up and cleared his throat as he pulled the chain on the lamp that sat on his nightstand. He glanced over his shoulder at his still-sleeping wife. Late night and early morning emergency calls for the sheriff were rare occasions around here. The sheriff's home was a quiet and peaceful one. The house had been built by Harlen's father, Charley, who had been one of the town's original firemen, when the volunteer fire department was first organized back in '58. Charley had also built the Pine Grove Baptist Church up on Rose Hill. He'd dug the basement with a pickax and a shovel, if you can believe that. Harlen had inherited Charley's large, broad stature, as well as his stern demeanor. The phone rang again.

"This better be good," the sheriff mumbled as he reached for the receiver.

5

SHERIFF JENKINS TURNED HIS CAR onto Kesler Hollow Road. The headlights brushed across the trees and cut into the dense fog. The dawn of the early morning had just begun to lift the darkness from the hills. It was that time of early morning when the battle between dark and light was still undecided.

The sheriff leaned forward in his seat. The anxiety over Lilly's disappearance that had been hibernating for seven years was now fully awake and hungry. He was up on his haunches. As he drove the cruiser up the road and closer to the Baldridges', the red and blue lights of his deputy's car became apparent, illuminating the breaking fog as it danced across the side of the Baldridge home. The eerie familiarity of the scene was not lost on the sheriff. He let out a deep breath as he brought his car to a stop in the driveway.

As soon as he stepped out, his deputy ran to greet him "She's in the living room, over by the fireplace."

"I gotta see this," the sheriff said as he made his way toward the steps of the wooden deck that led to the front door.

Inside the Baldridge place everything was eerily calm and peaceful. Mrs. Baldridge held her daughter in a blanket by the fire stove while Mrs. Baldridge's sister Patty, along with Patty's two daughters, were busy making tea and food and seeing that everything was so-so. *News tumbles down the family tree pretty fast around here*, the sheriff thought to himself as he entered the room.

"Mornin', Mrs. Baldridge," Sheriff Jenkins said as he removed his hat. He gazed down at the scene with reserved yet obvious wonderment. "Is she okay?" he asked after a brief pause.

"Y-y-yes." Nell's voice cracked as a tear ran down her face. She turned her head up toward the sheriff and looked him in the eyes. "She's just fine."

***

Ben and I just stood in the corner silently, taking it all in. We'd had a difficult night. The sheriff gave us a hard stare as he entered the house. He stood there motionless for a moment, just looking at Nell cuddling Lilly, before he spoke. "Tell me 'bout the Stillwater boy," the sheriff said without taking his eyes off the girl.

Just then Jimmy came in. "Sheriff, there's a stir starting out here. The emergency medical team is here, and some people have started gatherin' around wanting to know what's going on. They've heard something 'bout Lilly being found and ..."

"Just hold your horses, Jimmy. Let's get our own bearings first and just keep everyone outside for now."

The sheriff looked back over at me, expecting an answer about Hot Rod. "Sir, he's shot himself dead in that old barn down the road toward the Hayfields," I managed to choke out. "The same place we found Lilly."

The deputy stood next to the sheriff, anticipating his response.

"Take the emergency squad down there pronto, Jimmy."

Jimmy was as pale as a ghost. He glanced at Lilly and then at me and Ben, and then out the door he went.

The sheriff took his time in approaching Lilly as he listened to Ben and me recalling the events of the night. I'm not sure that he was even listening, to tell you the truth. Ben's mom was holding on to her daughter in the blanket, so I don't know if the sheriff saw it right off. I gotta say that Harlen Jenkins was a good man and a good sheriff. He never made rash decisions, and he was fair and polite with everyone.

He neared Lilly and Nell and knelt down on one knee, ever so slowly. "Is she injured at all, Nell?"

"No, Sheriff, it's a miracle from Heaven—my baby is home and well."

"Nell, I'm gonna have to let the EMTs come in and check her out, make an official report and all. But before I do, could I just get a better look at her and ask her a few questions?" You could tell that if it was left to Harlen, he would just as soon leave and let the family enjoy the moment.

***

Harlen Jenkins should be commended for the tact and restraint he displayed when he first got a full look at Lilly. I was looking directly at him when he saw her. His eyes couldn't hide his reaction—he was mortified. No one had worried themselves over the disappearance of Lilly Baldridge more than Sheriff Jenkins. I think when she vanished, he took it upon himself—a man on a mission, you might say—to find Lilly and bring peace back to Johnson County. And now here she sat, as big as you please. He remembered exactly what she looked like when she went missing, and he was staring at that exact same image right now.

"Lilly, are you hurt?" Sheriff Jenkins asked with a nervous but gentle voice.

She looked up at Harlen with an ambivalent glaze, but she didn't speak. I could tell this was unsettling to the sheriff. He turned to Nell.

"Where's Earl?" the sheriff asked.

Nell's pleasant demeanor immediately changed at the

mention of Earl. Ben's father had been the first to see us when we brought Lilly into the house an hour earlier.

He was a man of few words. It was as if Earl Baldridge had been given a set number of words when he was born, so when he chose to dispense them, he did so with great frugality. When you asked Earl for an opinion, it was like asking him to donate to charity or something. All the years I'd been hanging around their house, Earl must have spoken to me only a handful of times.

His reaction was the opposite of Nell's. During the first few moments of his reunion with Lilly, something had happened to deeply trouble Earl. I noticed the shift in his demeanor immediately and had since been keeping track of his actions. He had retreated into the dining room, and there he remained. That room featured in many of my memories of childhood. An easy chatter usually accompanied lunches and dinners taken there, and the walls were warm and cozy, like a hen's wings around her chicks. But now dread hung heavy in the room, voiding it of anything warm and cozy. An awkward distance now pervaded the space between Earl and the scene in the living room.

"He's having his coffee in the dining room," Nell answered flatly.

***

Earl Baldridge sat at the dining table with both hands cradling his cup of coffee, his eyes staring into emptiness.

"Earl, do you mind if I sit with you for a minute?" The sheriff had helped himself to the coffee, and now he pulled a chair from the table. He sat with a solemn reverence, and an uncomfortable moment passed.

"She used to call me Daddy," Earl said.

Harlen lifted his eyes and gazed at Earl, knowing that anything coming from him should be fully absorbed.

"Always Daddy. Now, after all this time, those boys find her and bring her home, and she looks at me and calls me Father."

Harlen and Earl just stared at each other. They weren't exactly what you'd call friends, and they weren't enemies either, but a tangible uneasiness existed between them.

"Harlen, I looked in her eyes, th-th-those eyes." A tear streamed down Earl's face from the flood of gloom that welled in his eyes. "That's not my little girl."

The sheriff just sat there looking at Earl for a moment, a deepening anxiety and concern in the pit of his stomach. He couldn't help thinking back to when she went missing. The days following her disappearance had been some of the worst days of Harlen Jenkins's life. He thought of Cristina, his daughter, who had been like a little sister to Lilly. He remembered the sympathy he'd felt for Earl as he imagined what it would be like if his own daughter had gone missing.

"Try to keep it together, Earl. I promise I'll get to the bottom of this." Just as the words tumbled out of Harlen's mouth, he remembered making a very similar promise to Earl seven years earlier. Both men held their stare. "You know I'm going to have to let the feds know she's been found, but I'll drag my feet on that as long as I can," the sheriff said as he stood from the table.

He approached the hallway and turned as if to speak again. Earl Baldridge was just staring at the empty chair where Harlen had sat. Sheriff Jenkins turned slowly and left the room.

***

When the sheriff entered the barn, he saw Deputy John Quills and EMT Billy Rayburn cautiously examining Rod's body. Nearby, EMT Randy Cooper was attempting to give aid to Jimmy Allen, who had passed out and bumped his noggin upon seeing the carnage.

"Oh my," the sheriff said quietly as he neared Rodney's body.

The sun was just starting to rise, but a heavy fog still lay in the hollow. The light coming through the windows and open spaces of the old barn was a steel blue mist. After a moment of silently peering at Rodney, the sheriff looked at Deputy Quills. "John, tape this whole barn off and don't let anybody get near it … and I mean anybody!"

"Yes, sir!" Like a bolt of lightning, Deputy John Quills was on the case.

The sheriff turned to Jimmy. "For goodness' sake, son, pull it together!"

"Okay, Sheriff, sorry," Jimmy said as he stood with a wobble.

"Get ahold of Doc Williams and help Quills." Doc Williams was Cripple Creek's only legally practicing physician, and he served as the county coroner as well.

As he strode toward the open gate of the barn, Harlen turned and pointed to the EMTs. "You two, go up and take a look at the girl. If there's nothing that needs immediate attention, pack up and leave!"

The sheriff turned and looked around the barn. The shadows of the deputies danced through the slats as they walked around the barn outside, taping off the scene. Harlen pulled both his weathered hands down his face and across the scruff of his chin. He had a feeling that he hadn't experienced in a long time—seven years, to be exact. He thought back to when Lilly had originally disappeared. He remembered the mayhem of the storm coupled with the frantic search. He could still hear the freight train roar of the storm tearing through the hollow, the screams of the people searching for Lilly, and the cacophony of breaking trees and limbs. Now new questions arose in his mind. Why had Rodney Stillwater shot himself? Why here? Why now? He once again found himself anchored in the anxiety of the unknown. And he knew that he had to call the last person on earth that he wanted to talk to.

6

FEDERAL AGENT TUCKER DAVIDSON RUBBED most everybody the wrong way. And Sheriff Jenkins was no exception. As a matter of fact, the sheriff had a *special* kind of dislike for Agent Davidson. Back in '79, he'd come struttin' into town like he was cock of the walk. He stepped on the sheriff's toes so many times that it eventually sent poor ole Harlen to the hospital for what appeared to be a nervous breakdown. Truth is, the sheriff had taken about as much as any good man could. At the end of the investigation, when the feds were packing up shop and leaving town, Sheriff Jenkins and Agent Davidson had to be pulled apart right out in front of the municipal building with what seemed like half the town watching. When Harlen went back into his office, he at once began to smash everything in sight. They say it took six grown men to wrestle him outta there.

Now here he was, as big as you please, Special Agent Tucker Davidson leading the cavalry, turning onto Main Street with another blacked-out sedan and something resembling an ambulance following behind. As he sat behind his desk, Harlen watched them all come pulling in. "What took you so long?" he muttered sarcastically. The Lexington office of the FBI was a two-hour drive from Cripple Creek, once you made it out to the highway, that is. The sheriff had figured it wouldn't take them long to arrive once he filled them in on the details, but this was impressively fast. The noonday sun had chased the autumn chill away, but when he saw the ambulance-type vehicle, a cold shiver ran through him, and he stood quickly, sending his chair crashing against the wall.

"What the ...?" Harlen murmured as he made his way to the front door. He immediately regretted telling Agent Davidson the whole story about Lilly.

***

Special Agent Davidson parked his government sedan close to the front, in Cripple Creek's only official handicap space. He opened the door and stood outside the car. For a minute he just stood there, looking up and down the street. Through the big glass windows on the front of the building, he could see Sheriff Jenkins nearing the front doors. Tucker adjusted his tie and under his breath said, "Take a swing at me this time, old man, and I'm going to ..."

7

THE BALDRIDGE PLACE WAS A stir of activity. Many relatives and friends had gathered in and around the house. Tommy's folks already had him out in the family truck, where they were giving him the twenty-questions routine. Some folks were hanging nearby to see if they could hear what he had to say. But Tommy had checked out. He hadn't said a word since we'd come carrying her up the road through the fog. He was deadpan. He had what my uncle John would've called "that space cadet glow."

Ben's driveway and half the side yard sat full of vehicles and people. Most everybody was being courteous and staying outside, but word had hit the crowd about her looking just like the same twelve-year-old girl whose disappearance had sent shockwaves of grief, worry, and fear throughout this little town seven years ago. There was indeed some fervent conversation going on.

Of course, my folks were there too. Mom was in the house doing what she could to help Nell, along with Ben's aunt Patty and her girls, and my dad sat in the dining room with Earl and Lester Hayfield. Lester was about the only person Earl talked to on a regular basis. I don't know if that was because they were good friends or because Lester was just the one who happened to live closest.

Ben and I retreated to Ben's bedroom. At first we just paced nervously around in small strange patterns.

"What just happened?" Ben finally said.

I knew how he felt. The whole thing seemed so surreal, and now that we were able to stop and process a bit, I was struck dumb. I just looked at Ben, slightly shaking my head with my mouth open and my hands out to my sides. I had no words. I returned to pacing the floor.

"What do we do?" he asked.

"She hasn't aged," I declared suddenly as I stopped and looked at Ben.

"I know," he whispered loudly as he stepped toward me.

I took a couple of steps and met him halfway. We looked each other in the eye. There wasn't a half-inch difference in our height, and we were both lean and wiry—the kind of lean and wiry that throwin' hay all day and chasing girls all night will get you.

We were in that peculiar whisper mode, you know, when you're whispering and nobody's around to hear it.

"And why was Rodney hollerin' out her name anyway?" I said.

"I know, *before* we found her."

"She hasn't said three words since we got her up here."

"She smiled at me," Ben said.

"Me too!"

"But I haven't seen her smile at anyone else, even Ma."

"You see the way she looked at the sheriff? Whoa."

"I know. That one made my short hairs stand up."

"But it's like she recognizes us."

"Maybe it's because we found her and brought her up here."

"Maybe."

"We should get something of hers and see if she recognizes it!"

"That's a good idea. Like what kind of thing?"

"I don't know."

"Let's go to her room and look for something."

As we turned to leave Ben's room, there was a frantic rap

on his window. Startled, we turned around and saw Cristina looking through the glass.

I ran to the window and threw open the bottom sash.

"Cristina," I said.

"Edison." She grabbed my shirt and pulled me close. We kissed long and slow.

"*Ahem!*" Ben blurted out after a few seconds.

I helped Cristina through the window. It had been a while since we'd kissed like that, and I gotta tell ya, it felt pretty darn good.

"Is she really here?" Cristina asked.

"Yeah," Ben answered.

"And does she really look ..."

"Yep, sure does!" I cut her off before she could finish.

***

Cristina went directly to the living room to see Lilly for herself, while Ben and I darted into Lilly's old bedroom. Nell had kept everything just as it was when Lilly went missing. She couldn't bear the notion of packing everything up or changing things around. The door to Lilly's room had mostly remained closed over the past seven years. It was a little time capsule of better times.

"How about some of her old notebooks or schoolbooks?" I asked as I leafed through a stack of old school material.

"That's good, but I'm looking for something specific," Ben said without even looking at my finds.

I turned to see him over in the closet, reaching back behind a stack of boxes.

"It should be right here." Frustration filled Ben's voice as he frantically flailed his hand about blindly behind the boxes. "Got it!" he finally exclaimed.

"Got wha ..." I started to ask, just as he stretched out his hand, holding Lilly's diary. "Perfect!" I said.

We crept quietly back into the living room, though it wasn't like we really needed to be quiet; this was the most noise I'd ever heard around this place. When Ben showed Lilly her diary, she smiled at him again. He started to open it up and show her some pages, and she gently reached out and clamped the diary shut with her hand. This made me giggle a bit, and when I did, she snapped around and looked at me.

The moment started to freak me out, but then she smiled at me and let out a little giggle. Cristina and Nell laughed too. It was a nice moment that took a bit of the tension out of the air.

We heard a commotion outside. Ben and I ran to the kitchen 'cause the window in there had the best view of the driveway. What we saw horrified us. "The feds!" I cried out. In the line of cars, which the sheriff's car was leading, I saw the black ambulance and knew that wasn't good. I figured the sheriff had to let the feds know what exactly was going on. I felt a knot in my stomach again. They were going to take her.

The sheriff jumped out of his car almost before it stopped and immediately put up his hands and started yellin' something to the crowd of family and friends that had gathered around over the past few hours. The folks 'round here hadn't trusted the FBI before any of this happened, so you can imagine how they felt about them now. He had everybody's attention for about a half second. That's when the two black sedans and the ambulance vehicle came sliding up, each sending a large dust cloud into the air.

Ben turned toward the dining room and hollered, "Hey, Pa, the feds are here again!"

Earl calmly stood up, walked over to the gun cabinet, pulled out a pistol, and tucked it in the back of his pants. He walked past us toward the kitchen door. He turned before going outside and said, "Watch the girl."

"Yes, sir," we said in unison.

We immediately ran to the living room, where Nell was hovering over Lilly.

"What ... what's all the fuss outside?" asked Patty. Ben's aunt and her girls were still minding the shop, but everyone was on edge.

"Pretty soon all that fuss is gonna end up in here," I said under my breath as I shot Ben a worried look.

Cristina ran to the window to see what was going on. I followed, and outside we saw her dad, the sheriff. Cristina looked concerned as her eyes passed over the scene. I then followed her gaze to the pistol jutting out of the back of Earl's pants as he approached the agents. The tension was palpable. She turned and looked at me. "Eddie, this doesn't look good."

The unease inside the house worsened as everyone looked toward the front door. The commotion was growing outside. I could hear the sheriff's voice. Ben and I looked at each other, both of us knowing the moment to act was upon us. Together we moved toward Lilly.

"Kitchen door!" Ben blurted out.

Nell wore a look of fright and confusion on her face as we quickly came toward her. Reluctantly, she released custody of Lilly.

"Lil, we need to move," I said as I gently grabbed her arm. She hopped up and stood beside me with a quirky little smile, like I'd just asked her if she'd like to go for some ice cream or something. Whatever our plan was, she was on board.

***

The bustle around Sheriff Jenkins and Agent Tucker resembled an agitated bees' nest. The finer points of jurisdiction were being heatedly debated between the two men. Seemed like they were pickin' right back up where they'd left off seven years ago. Deputies John Quills and Jimmy Allen had also returned from the barn and were trying, unsuccessfully, to calm the scene. The crowd made its way to the front porch.

Sheriff Jenkins quickly ascended the first few steps and turned with his hands in the air. "Now everybody just hang on a daggum minute!" he shouted. A quick hush fell over the mob, as if the judge's gavel had fallen. Harlen Jenkins operated on about as steady a keel as anyone, but when he demanded attention, he got it. He once had been the middle linebacker for the town's high school football team and hadn't allowed a single touchdown all of his senior season. At fifty-seven years of age, he was still an intimidating figure when he decided to be.

"I know you all are just trying to be protective and lookin' out for Earl and his family here, and that's just fine, but we're gonna have to let Agent Davidson and his people here take a look at things." Tucker was accompanied by two other agents and what appeared to be a medical team.

"Everybody just calm down and give us a little space here so the agents can do their job and be on their way." The sheriff looked down at Davidson as he said the last part, their eyes locking. Harlen was standing his ground the best he could.

After a moment, Harlen turned so that Agent Davidson and his people could move up on the porch and toward the front door.

"Quills, get up here and watch the door, and Jimmy, try to keep everyone calm, will ya?" Harlen said, warily looking about the scene as he turned to go inside the house. He was nervous as a cat to see how Agent Tucker would react to seeing Lilly, as he should be. Tucker Davidson had the personality of a stomach ulcer. The sheriff had already revealed the particulars of the past twelve hours to the agent, but you never really know how someone is gonna react to something truly bizarre until they see it for themselves, ya know. Funny, though—it turned out it didn't matter.

8

B EN TURNED THE KNOB OF the back door by the kitchen with the hand of a seasoned safecracker. Barely a hinge or door around the old farmhouse moved without a squeaky protest. Ben's granddad had built this place before there was even running water out in these parts. Luckily, the unwelcomed ruckus coming through the front door was more than enough to drown out the little bit of noise we were making.

"Easy does it," I whispered as we quietly emerged into the backyard that had just moments ago been busy with people gathered around. But the scene out front had conveniently rendered the yard empty. The yard stretched out to the cornfield and the surrounding hills.

"Through the field and into the woods," Ben said as he pointed toward the hills. He was holding on to Lilly's hand, but she really didn't need any leading. She seemed to know what was going on. I took a couple of steps to the edge of the house and peeked around to the front yard. I could hear heated discussion out front, but the only person I could see was Deputy Jimmy Allen. He was standing off to the side against the big oak tree that provided shade for half the house. He looked helpless and full of frustration, his attention fully focused on the mob. Luckily, the only person who could have seen us crossing the yard seemed genuinely distracted.

We made our break for the cornfield. Dashing the open

hundred-foot distance, I felt that sense of crossing the point of no return. Ben and I had pulled off our fair share of tomfoolery in our day, but we had never descended to the level of criminal. The gravity of what we were doing surged over me.

I was in front, leading the charge. I glanced back at Ben, who looked like he had just robbed the henhouse as he pulled Lilly along, the sun illuminating the long blonde locks flowing behind her. I shot a glance over at Jimmy just as I slipped into a row of cornstalks. He was looking right at us. He dropped the cup of water he was holding, lifting his hand to point at us.

"Hey!" I heard Jimmy yell.

I broke into a full gallop as Ben shouted, "Go, go!" The cat was out of the bag.

My eyes were wide and my heart pounded as I churned through the corn leaves that littered each row. *So much for being sneaky*, I thought. I was trying not to get disoriented and to just stay in the same row. It was the end of the season, so the corn was at full height, about eight or ten feet. Even in the daytime the slant light of the hollow made it seem eerily dark in some parts of the field. The field was about one hundred yards long, but you never saw the light at the end until you were right upon it. So it seemed to go on forever.

I looked back to make sure I wasn't losing Ben and Lilly, with both arms up and out in front of me to deflect the scratchy leaves. I was trying to form some sort of plan in my head. We couldn't just play hide-and-seek around the Baldridge place. We had to put some distance between us and them.

I knew that just beyond the cornfield lay the vast hill country and the labyrinth of game trails, paths, and dirt roads to choose from. Ben and I knew this country well, but the question was which way to go.

9

AGENT DAVIDSON BURST THROUGH THE front door, looking left and right. Curiosity had overcome him. Nell, Patty, and the girls sat nervously in the living room, apparently startled by the abrupt invasion. Agent Davidson's anticipation of this moment had been lost, nearly forgotten over the years as his caseload of missing persons fogged the memory of Lilly Baldridge. But now he had a chance for redemption of his first case that had gone sour.

"Where's the girl?" Tucker Davidson demanded with a great deal of expectation.

He received only blank, silent stares from the women. The timid response immediately alarmed the agent; something was awry. He turned to Sheriff Jenkins.

"What's going on here, Sheriff?" He glared at the small host of people that had followed Harlen into the house.

Everyone looked around at one another, waiting for somebody to break the silence. The sheriff saw Cristina standing in the hallway and shot her a stern look. She knew what that look meant: *What's going on here, young lady?* She shrugged her shoulders as her gaze drifted to the floor.

"Hey!" The yell drifted in through an open window. Davidson saw Jimmy Allen dart past one window and then the next, toward the backyard.

Agent Davidson sprang across the room like a lion to its prey and plastered his face to the glass of a back window, both hands

41

grasping the wooden jambs. The girls let out a startled scream. And in the next moment, Agent Davidson let out a surprised gasp. The girl's blonde hair, lit up by the sun, flew behind her as she ran. He felt the hair on the back of his neck rise as he caught a fleeting glimpse of Lilly vanishing into the cornfield.

THE FIRST THING THAT CAME to my mind as we cleared the cornfield and stood at the edge of the woods, our hearts racing and our lungs screaming for air, was Throttle. He lived out of the way in a nice little spread at the end of Butler Hollow. His dad was Doc Williams, the same Doc Williams who was currently transporting poor ole Hot Rod to the county morgue. Getting there would require a few miles of running through the hills and over the ridges, but this would provide ample time and space to shake off anybody who might be tryin' to chase us—namely, Deputy Jimmy Allen. That boy sure wasn't the sharpest tool in the shed, but he could run through the hills with the best of 'em. I guess you're just kinda born that way around these parts. But he wasn't as familiar with this neck of the woods as we were, so we were able to shake him loose about the time we ducked into the top of Butler Hollow.

We stopped just under the ridgeline in a little clearing where some trees had blown down. We could make out the Williams homestead from where we sat.

Ben slumped against a felled tree, catching his breath. "I figured this was where we were headed." He spat on the ground.

"Yeah, I figured Doc Williams would be busy with ... well, ya know."

"Yeah."

"And Throttle is probably sleepin' like the dead down in

the basement. You know that boy won't stir till at least the afternoon."

Throttle Williams was a good friend of ours. He was a year older and a grade ahead of us in school, but he would always pick us up when we were out walking somewhere and give us a ride. Once he snuck us into the drive-in theater in the trunk of his car. We thought he was so cool. Of course his name wasn't really Throttle. His name was William—that's right, William Williams. But when he was eight years old, he had managed to hot-wire the family car and crash it into the side of their house. His granddaddy had started calling him Throttle that very day, and it stuck. From that day forward, he was Throttle Williams. That same year, his mom decided to run off with some magician from the county fair who came through every year. Throttle changed during that time. All he would do was work on his cars and engines. I think it was a defense mechanism or somethin', like he totally changed who he was to avoid dealing with the pain of his mama up and leaving the way she did.

When Lilly disappeared all those years ago, he had really bonded with Ben, like he knew what it was like to have someone taken from your life. I guess that's why Throttle was always giving us rides everywhere. He had a connection with us. And I guess that's why we ended up running to his place. I knew we could trust him.

"Throttle," Lilly suddenly said.

Ben and I both looked at her. She hadn't made a peep since we'd taken off through the cornfield.

She had a girlish smile on her face. I looked closer at her. "You remember Throttle, Lil?"

She just smiled and looked at me for a moment. "Throttle can take us to find her," she said bluntly.

Ben and I looked at each other. Her words had stopped us both in our tracks.

"Find who, sis?" Ben asked.

She turned to Ben and reached out her arm to him. In her hand was the diary.

II

DEPUTY JIMMY ALLEN EMERGED FROM the cornfield into the Baldridges' backyard. He had his hat off and both hands on his knees. He was breathing heavily with a look of defeat on his face.

"I lost 'em, Sheriff. I don't know what those boys were thinking, but they sure didn't slow down, and they got the girl with 'em. What are they thinking, pullin' a stunt like that?"

"Just calm down, Jimmy," the sheriff said as he walked through the yard with everyone following behind.

"Those boys are now kidnappers on top of obstructing a federal investigation!" Tucker Davidson shouted. He stormed back and forth across the yard. He stopped and pointed at the sheriff. "If you have anything to do with this charade ..."

Harlen took two long strides toward Davidson and put his finger in the agent's face. "It was you who spooked them, pulling up here like that!"

The men continued screaming at each other although they were only inches apart. Things were getting tense in a hurry. The other agents were closing in to back up Agent Davidson. Deputy John Quills moved in to support the sheriff, along with Lester Hayfield and Earl Baldridge.

Patty and the girls were now out in the yard screaming too. Jimmy Allen just stood there and stared at the whole scene, helpless. Accusations, threats, and curses were being thrown about by all parties involved. The Baldridge backyard had descended into anarchy.

12

WE APPROACHED THE HOUSE CAREFULLY. Doc Williams's car was gone, but Throttle's '73 Dodge Charger was parked in its usual spot. Man, that car was a rocket. Throttle had it souped up and running at the edge of its capacity. It roared through the back roads of Cripple Creek, and you could hear it from miles away.

Now we were sneaking past it and moving toward the house. When we arrived at the side door by the garage, we climbed up the steps, and I banged my knuckles on the aluminum storm door.

We waited. But all was silent around the house. I reached up again and rapped harder on the door. Throttle was taking forever. *Come on!* I thought. Nervously, I glanced down the driveway, dreading the sight of a car.

Finally, I heard a stir inside the house—footsteps. "Throttle!" I said in a loud hush.

The rattle of the lock caused us to take a step back. Throttle swung the door open and raised his hand to deflect the sunlight away from his still-sleepy eyes. "What are you guys ..."

"Hi, Throttle!" Lilly cheerfully blurted out.

Throttle's eyes went wide, and he quickly took two steps backward, crashed into the coat rack, and fell over. Throttle, the adrenaline junky, fainted.

13

SHERIFF JENKINS AND AGENT DAVIDSON laid the map of Johnson County across the hood of Deputy Jimmy Allen's car. It was the best the sheriff could produce. It was a topographical map, but it showed all the state, county, and township roads, most of which were dirt and gravel. Agent Davidson slammed his finger on the map.

"Your boy lost them here. Where are they running to?" Agent Davidson demanded.

Jimmy Allen stood next to the car by the sheriff. He looked at the sheriff briefly, gritting his teeth, and looked away. His pride was hurting.

Harlen resisted the urge to tear into Agent Davidson. "That's Butler Hollow. A few folks live along the road that runs up there, and Doc Williams has his place at the end. He's the one that carried the Stillwater boy outta here this morning."

"Any reason they headed that way?"

"Now how am I supposed to know what those boys are thinkin'?"

Jimmy Allen leaned toward the pair. "Don't those boys run around with Throttle?"

Agent Davidson stood up straight and looked at the sheriff. "Who's Throttle?"

"That's Doc Williams's boy," the sheriff said bluntly as he moved to open the driver's door of his cruiser. "Jimmy, come with me. Quills, you stay with the agents here and see that they

49

have all they need." Harlen slid into his seat and had the car moving backward and around the federal vehicles so quickly that Jimmy nearly got left behind. Harlen wanted to take care of this on his own.

But Davidson wasn't about to let him. He ordered the rest of his team to stay with Deputy Quills and jumped in his black sedan. He stomped on the gas and slung the car around right in the middle of the driveway and took off to follow the sheriff.

14

WE WERE ALL SITTING AGAINST the wall of Throttle's garage sipping on Pepsis. It had been a long night for us. We had filled Throttle in on what was going on after he came to, and he was letting it all sink in.

"I always knew ole Hot Rod was a little off, but ... *wow!*" Throttle said as he ran his hands through his long red hair. "I can't believe she's sitting right here ... looking like ..." Throttle trailed off, without the words to describe the anomaly he was seeing.

I was sitting next to Lilly, who was draining the last bit of soda out of her can. She sat up straight, put a serious look on her face, and let out a loud belch. We all laughed, and Ben clapped his hands. "Way to go, sis!"

Lilly raised her fingers to her mouth and giggled.

I noticed the diary lying there beside her. I felt inquisitive. I glanced at Lilly as I picked it up and leafed through some pages. She gave me a warm smile that washed away any trepidation I had about picking it up. I began to read.

> *May 23, 1979*
> *Well, the school year is almost finished and I am so excited for the summer. Bible Camp this year will be even better than last. I just love this time of year in Cripple Creek. Everyone seems to come alive a little more. The swap meet will*

*be out at the fairgrounds next week, and I plan
on working at the church booth making snow
cones. I'm also glad that the Hilltop Jamboree
has started back up again on Friday nights. I just
love going up there to listen to the banjos and
gospel music. But, I'm nervous up there more
and more. He touched me again last Friday.
And those things he whispers at me, they are so
disgusting and I don't even know what most of
it means. I'm afraid to tell anyone because it's
just so dirty, and if nobody would believe me,
they would just think I was like one of those girls
always going to the drive-in to be with boys.*

I felt like I'd been kicked in the chest. "Lilly!" I turned to
look at her. "Who are you talking about here on this page?"

She looked at me with all seriousness. "She's talking about
Stillwater."

"Whoa, back up!" Throttle interjected. "*She?*"

"That's kinda the way she's been talking, Throttle," I
said.

"For real. In the third person?" he asked.

"For real," I said.

Ben sat up and took notice. "Let me see."

I handed the diary to Ben and looked back to Lilly. "Are you
talking about Rodney—Hot Rod?"

Lilly maintained her somber expression and shook her head
no.

I continued to look at her, a lump in my throat. "Who
then?"

"His father," she whispered.

15

THE TWO VEHICLES DASHED ACROSS Main Street. A whirlwind of dust, gravel, dirt, and asphalt showed the after-burn of the dusty rocket that sped through town and out toward Fairgrounds Road. Tucker Davidson was tailing the sheriff as if he were in a race. His hands gripped the steering wheel so tight that his knuckles were white. The only reason he wasn't out in front was that he had no idea where he was; he had to follow Sheriff Jenkins, and that put him through the roof.

They were on their way to the Williams place at the back of Butler Hollow. Sheriff Jenkins swallowed hard as he drove his cruiser through the back roads of Johnson County at speeds reminiscent of the whiskey runs that had taken place during Prohibition. He'd driven out to Doc Williams's place many times, but not at this furious pace.

What was causing all this stir was the girl, Lilly. He'd seen her with his own eyes, just hours before. Yet still she was elusive, like a thief in the night. Harlen had lost her once, and now the chance of redemption was close. He wanted nothing more than to simply return her to her family. But now it felt like he was on board an out-of-control freight train. The jumbled events of the past twelve hours replayed in his mind.

"Watch out, Sheriff!" Jimmy yelled from the passenger seat.

Harlen swerved to miss a large oak branch that had fallen across the road. The rear end of the car swayed back and forth as the tires lost traction—Harlen was doing everything he could to keep it between the ditches. Jimmy yelled out as they narrowly missed going into the creek on the right side of the road. But the sheriff steered out of it like a pro.

Agent Davidson wasn't so fortunate. Trailing so close behind the sheriff's car, he didn't have time to react. He slammed into the branch full force, sending splinters, wood chips, leaves, and dirt into the air. His government sedan was rendered lame, a tree limb driven through the radiator. Steam and dust coughed from the wreckage.

The sheriff's patrol car had stopped sideways in the road. Harlen jumped out of the car and threw his hat down on the road with one great swing of his burly arm. "Daggumit!" he bellowed.

Jimmy slowly emerged from the cruiser with wobbly legs. Meanwhile, in the disabled government sedan, Agent Davidson moaned groggily as he sat back in the driver's seat.

The sheriff approached the wreckage. "Davidson, you alright?"

The agent looked up at the sheriff with contempt. "Yeah, Harlen, just peachy," he said sarcastically. Blood trickled out of his nose and mouth, but his injuries were not serious. "Now get me out of this heap!"

16

"HIS FATHER?" I SAID TO Lilly.

She nodded.

I turned and looked at Ben. "His father?" I repeated.

"Harold Stillwater," Throttle said. "That's one mean old man."

I turned again to Lilly. "Harold Stillwater, is that who the diary is talking about?"

Once again she nodded. We all looked at each other with confusion in our eyes and on our faces.

"If it was him," Ben said, "then why did Hot Rod flip out and ... you know?" Ben didn't even want to say the words.

"Maybe he was inculpate," Throttle blurted out.

"Inculpate?" I asked. "Where in the wide world of sports did you pick up that word?"

Throttle shrugged. "The television, I guess."

The truth is, Throttle was probably one of the smartest people I knew. He'd gotten straight As in high school, and they'd wanted to make him valedictorian. He flatly refused. Said he didn't want to send out the wrong message, whatever he meant by that. But that was Throttle, an enigma.

As we were all standing there pondering the heavy questions, Throttle lifted his head. "You ever been out to the Stillwater place? Creepy if you ask me."

The Stillwater place was indeed creepy. Rodney's mom died

when he was a young'un, and Harold Stillwater wasn't any more fit to raise a child than Ted Bundy. Old Man Stillwater and his boy were highly dysfunctional, even by Cripple Creek standards.

17

THE SHERIFF HAD NEEDED TO get his tire iron out of the back of his cruiser to pry open the door of the sedan. But though Davidson was shaken up, he was okay to go. Now the three of them were driving up the road toward the Williams homestead with Agent Davidson riding shotgun and Jimmy in the back. They came in sight of the house.

"Looks mighty quiet," Jimmy muttered from the backseat.

"Too quiet," the sheriff added.

Sheriff Jenkins slowed the cruiser as he approached the gravel driveway. All eyes were on the Williams home. It wasn't anything special, considering Doc Williams made as good a living as anyone around these parts. The home had belonged to the doctor's parents, and it was the only house he'd ever lived in. But the garage *was* something special. It wasn't much to look at, but it was what was on the inside that made it unique. It was a large rectangular metal building larger than the house, and in it was a '55 Chevy, a '57 Chevy, and a '33 Ford Model A. All of them breathed fire. And, of course, there was Throttle's Dodge Charger, which now sat in the driveway between the house and the garage.

"Looks like Throttle's home," Jimmy exclaimed as he patted Agent Davidson on the shoulder and pointed. "That's his car right there."

The sheriff eased the car up close to Throttle's Dodge and put the cruiser in park. The three men exited the car and cautiously made their way to the front door. It was dead silent around the place, which made the sheriff uneasy.

Harlen rapped his beefy knuckles on the door. Jimmy took a deep breath. They remained silent as they strained to hear any stir in the house.

But as the two locals waited, Davidson suddenly raised his fist and beat on the door with the soft part of his hand.

"Mr. Throttle, this is the FBI. Open up!"

***

I hunkered down, trying to become one with the floorboard of Throttle's car. Ben was in the back with Lilly, doing the same. Beside me, Throttle was busy pulling wires down from under the dash. In this moment of crisis, we'd realized that we were sitting in the fastest car in Johnson County without a key to start it. We'd taken cover in the closest available spot when we heard the sheriff's car coming around the bend, which happened to be Throttle's ride. We all instinctively ducked down and laid low while the sheriff's car pulled up right next to us. The fox was in the henhouse. We all became ghosts as the three men emerged from the vehicle. All one of them had to do was come over and look into Throttle's car, and it would be game over. But fortune was on our side, and they moved toward the Williams family's front door.

"I'm stealing my own car," Throttle whispered.

"Yeah, classic—now hurry up and get us out of here," Ben said from the back. My stomach churned from the anticipation.

Suddenly the car's motor came to life; Throttle had found the right wires. There was no more wondering where we were among the officers. I quickly sat up to see where the posse was. They were still standing at the door, startled and frozen by the sudden roar of the engine.

It was kinda funny, the four of us looking at the three of them. For one golden moment while Throttle put the car in gear, we all seemed perplexed at the presence of the other group, like some grand discovery of a new tribe in the Amazon or somethin'.

Then Agent Davidson broke into a dead run straight at us. Throttle hit the accelerator, throwing dust and gravel everywhere. The rear end of the Charger swerved back and forth for a moment before catching traction. Tucker Davidson came within five feet of the car as it sped out of the driveway. Lilly sat up on her knees and looked out the back window at her pursuer. The agent's eyes locked on Lilly's as he ran after the car. This was the first close look Davidson had gotten of Lilly. The hair on the back of his neck stood up again, and the skin on his arms and hands tingled as he stopped running. He stood still for a moment and watched Lilly's face disappear into the dust and exhaust of the Dodge as it rushed from the driveway and onto the road.

***

If you've never been in the car with Throttle Williams when he is in a hurry to get somewhere, then you're missing out on a unique and terrifying experience. Some people are born with a certain gift, or inclination, you might say. Some are born with musical genius, and others might be destined to split the atom, but Throttle was born to burn rubber, pure and simple.

We raced down the driveway and onto the road. I firmly grasped the dashboard with both hands as Throttle let out a loud whoop. I wasn't really worried about the sheriff and Agent Davidson giving pursuit; my eyes were fixed forward. I heard Ben yelling over the roar of the engine to Lilly, "Hold on, sis!"

I glanced back at Ben and saw probably the exact look that was on my face. It's that look you have right before the roller coaster crests the first big drop.

As we came around the first big turn in the road, I saw the wreckage. I don't know whether I let out a scream or not, but

I immediately felt doomed. Throttle tapped the brakes, and the rear end of the Charger quickly swayed left. The turn in the road went sharply to the right, and the mass of timber and sedan occupied all of the right side of the road and most of the left. On the left side was a narrow shoulder that sloped directly into the creek that ran alongside Butler Hollow. Lilly let out a loud shriek from the back. Throttle was back into the gas and steering into the turn. I felt the back end of the car dip over the shoulder and into the creek as the front end clipped the ends of the branch that blocked our way. The Charger rocked violently as water, dust, and gravel filled the air. It crossed my mind that this, here and now, might be the end of our little adventure. Then the back end of the car caught traction and whipped to the right. I slammed full force into the passenger-side door as the Charger jumped from the creek and onto the road.

We continued racing down the road in shock and awe. It took me a moment to register that we had actually made it through.

Finally, Ben broke the silence with a yell filled with both elation and horror. "Wha-ooo-ah!" Ben had one hand on Throttle's shoulder and the other on mine. "That sure was some piece of drivin'!"

I glanced back over the seat at Lilly. "You okay, Lil?" She nodded with a nervous smile.

Throttle gripped the steering wheel and let out a big sigh. I think this was the first time he'd ever really scared himself. He looked at me and asked a very difficult question. "Where to now, Ed?"

We all looked out the back window of the Charger. We knew the sheriff and that hair-trigger Davidson would soon be on our tail.

18

THE SLEEPY TOWN OF CRIPPLE Creek had become a stir of activity. The locals were once again alive with speculation and concern over the events of the past day. The upset was eerily reminiscent of the disposition that had fallen over the town seven years earlier. Of course, the story was different depending on who you talked to. Some said she actually appeared younger than the twelve-year-old girl who had long ago disappeared, and some concluded that it was impossible, an illusion, a result of the senses being deceived in the heat of the moment.

And then there was Rodney. Some had heard that he had actually been killed by Lilly, who had come back from the dead, in league with Lucifer. You have to understand that a lot of folks in Cripple Creek were steeped in the old-time religion. For many, everything in life had a religious—and some might say superstitious—overtone. The folks out at the Community of the Redeemer church just outside of town even handled rattlesnakes in their Thursday night service. That's downright creepy if you ask me. The old-timers who gathered at Carl's Gas-n-Garage sat around recounting the events of the original disappearance of Lilly years ago while the younger crowd gathered in the parking lot of the high school. Many were unnerved by the incident.

Much attention was focused on the police station, which sat conspicuously quiet. Earlier, the coroner and Harold Stillwater had been spotted arriving at the building, with Mr. Stillwater obviously there to identify the body of his son. The most popular spot in town by far was DeeDee's Diner, since it was right across the street from the municipal building and all. There, folks could have their coffee, speculate about the goings-on, and keep an eye on the sheriff's office all at the same time.

So when Deputy John Quills pulled up in his police cruiser along with the government vehicles containing the rest of Agent Davidson's team, you can imagine the shake-up it caused. Everyone in DeeDee's Diner stood and moved toward the front of the restaurant, where the large plate glass window provided an unobstructed view of Main Street, and some spilled out onto the sidewalk. John Quills stepped out of his cruiser and pulled the brim of his hat low on his forehead as the agents made their way up the steps of the municipal building. He glanced over his shoulder at the gathering mob.

"Hey, John, where's Lilly?" someone shouted from the crowd.

That was the spark that started the fire. Suddenly the people of Cripple Creek wanted answers.

"Where's the sheriff?" someone yelled.

"Is she alive?" another called.

Soon it became mayhem, and Quills couldn't get up the steps fast enough to escape the throng of townsfolk. He wished the sheriff were here.

19

"DID YOU SEE THAT?" BEN asked from the backseat. "The fed crashed on the way up the hollow."

"Yeah," Throttle said. "The sheriff must've scooped him up and come right on after us."

"We have to find someplace to go!" I was in a panic. We needed to find a destination and quick.

"The bottoms!" Ben yelled above the roar of the wind and engine.

The river bottoms were the lowlands that wound with the river through the hills. Many cornfields occupied these flatlands because of the fertile soil provided by the river. There were a few homes here and there, but it wasn't what you would call prime real estate. The bottoms were prone to flooding, and the humidity was more oppressive near the river. The bottoms provided a good home for water moccasins, copperheads, snapping turtles, and spiders the size of your hand. Numerous roads crisscrossed through it, so it provided good little hiding places here and there if you needed a spot to make out with your girl or knock back a six-pack of Old Milwaukee. Ben and I knew the bottoms well. We had spent many a night down there fishing for big channel catfish or just hanging out, standing around a fire. These were some of the places where we could find solitude, so the bottoms seemed a good place to hide out.

"Yeah," Throttle said, nodding. "But we gotta shake the tail off us."

Ben reached over the seat and grabbed my shoulder. "And we gotta figure out what it is we're gonna do, Ed!"

"We need to find her!" Lilly suddenly exclaimed. We all turned and looked at her as Throttle sped down Butler Hollow.

"Stillwater's cellar," Lilly muttered.

Ben, Throttle, and I all looked at each other.

20

QUILLS WAS CERTAINLY GLAD TO be inside the sheriff's office. The other members of Davidson's team had already gone downstairs to the morgue, presumably to look at Rodney's body. The deputy took the chance to radio the sheriff.

"Sheriff, this is Quills. Come in. Over." There was a static pause.

"Yeah, John, whatcha got there? Over."

"There's a mighty mess of people out in front of the office wanting answers." The nervousness in Deputy Quills's voice was palpable. "And the federal agents are going about business like I'm not even here. They're already downstairs in the morgue, and I'm up here trying to keep the whole town from overtaking the building, and ..."

"Now just slow down there, Deputy. We're in pursuit of them boys right now, so just hang tight, and as soon as we round them up, we'll be on our way back there. Over."

"Okay, Sheriff, but hurry! Things are getting a little out of control here. Over."

"Alright, Quills. Lock the front doors so we don't get a crowd of locals in the office, and go down and see what's going on in the morgue ... and John ..."

"Yes, Sheriff."

"Don't let Doc Williams know just yet that his boy is out

there aiding and abetting them boys and Lilly. Just keep that under your hat for now. Over."

"Will do, Sheriff. Over."

***

When Quills went downstairs, he walked into a situation that had headed south. He could see Doc Williams doing his best to calm down Harold Stillwater and remove him from the room that contained his son's body.

Harold Stillwater pressed back against the doctor, pointing into the room.

"I'm taking my boy home today! I don't give a diddily damn what kinda tests and procedures you wanna do. That's my boy, and I'm taking him!"

Quills rushed down the hallway to assist Doc Williams because Mr. Stillwater was now in a full-on rage. The deputy grabbed Stillwater around the chest and pulled him away from the doorway and into the hall. As he did, he saw the agents gathered around Hot Rod's body. They were taking skin, blood, and hair samples. John Quills and Doc Williams gave each other an uneasy look.

"Agents!" Doc Williams said. "How about you just cease with your activities until I've had a chance to inspect the body? I believe this is my jurisdiction!" But the agents shut and locked the door without a word of explanation. Deputy Quills let go of Harold Stillwater, who slumped to the floor in defeat. The deputy banged his fist on the door to the morgue.

"You're overstepping your bounds here, agents!" shouted Quills. "This here is our building, and I'm telling you to open this door right now!" He beat his bony knuckles on the door once again.

"That's my office, Quills. Here's the key," the doc said as he rifled through a large set of keys and found the one for the morgue.

Quills tried the key, but it wouldn't turn the lock. "It's been jammed from the other side," he said.

Doc Williams started to turn to Harold Stillwater. "Hey, Harold, give us a ..." But Harold wasn't there.

***

Upstairs on the ground floor Harold Stillwater calmly walked to the locked front doors of the municipal building, where a dozen people were looking to get in. He unlatched the lock and let the big glass doors swing inward.

"What's going on here, Harold?" Bubba Spriggs was the first to enter the sheriff's office. He was still wearing his apron, greasy from fryin' up specials all afternoon in DeeDee's kitchen. As the rest of the crowd made its way into the lobby, everyone looked around and took in the emptiness of the sheriff's office.

"What's going on here?" Big Walt Miller demanded as he stepped through the crowd wearing nothing but his bib overalls and a ragged John Deere hat, his booming voice echoing through the building. Big Walt had been in DeeDee's all morning drinking coffee and getting himself riled up by the recent events.

"Deputy Quills and Doc Williams are contending with the feds downstairs at the morgue as we speak," said Stillwater. "They got themselves locked in there with my boy!"

This got the contingency of townsfolk riled up, and they moved toward the stairs. "Feds ain't gonna screw with us this time!" Walt blurted out as they made their way down the hall.

Once they were downstairs, Sam Bonner, Cripple Creek's one and only attorney, turned back and said, "We'll straighten this out for you, Harold, so you can ..."

Harold Stillwater once again slipped the scene. By this time he was slinking into his old pickup and backing out of his parking spot at the municipal building. He furtively dropped the shifter into drive and rolled away without looking back.

21

WE REACHED THE INTERSECTION OF Butler Hollow and Fairgrounds Road and heard the siren from the sheriff's car. Throttle turned left toward the river and away from town. As we tore down the road, I could see the sheriff's car racing down Butler Hollow behind us. My heart was racing, and my head was spinning. For a moment I thought about ending this situation, which had gotten way out of control. I started thinking about what kind of charges were going to be leveled against us, and for a moment my heart began to fail me. But I felt an overwhelming compulsion to see this through. Deep down I felt like what we were doing was right, as crazy and out of control as it had become. Something compelled me to hold fast.

"We can lose them in the bottoms!" I shouted at Throttle.

He just nodded a little and kept the pedal to the metal. We had to be putting distance between us and them because we were riding in a rocket driven by the most talented driver in the county. Nobody could drive like Throttle. He'd been racing go-carts at racetracks all across Kentucky since he was a kid. He had boxes filled with trophies and awards, but he didn't set them out on display like some folks do; Throttle was humble about his skills.

I turned to look behind us, and Throttle suddenly hit the brakes. The car decelerated at a terrific rate. I slammed full force into the front console and Ben and Lilly were plastered to the back of the front seat. We skidded for what seemed like a mile before we came to a stop. I looked up through the front windshield and beheld a big ole dairy cow. She was just standing there in the middle of the road like nobody's business, looking at us like we were nothin' special. Throttle honked his horn, but the cow just stood there. I jumped out of the car and ran full speed at the cow's behind, slamming my shoulder into her rump.

"Move, cow!" I screamed as I pushed with all my might. To my right I felt another body hit the cow. It was Ben. She finally started moving across the road. I looked back at the car and the road behind us. I could see the sheriff's cruiser about a mile up the road. As we inched the cow further, Throttle drove over into the ditch and barely around us.

"Get in! Get in!" he yelled. Ben and I dislodged ourselves from the cow and jumped in the car. Throttle tore away from the scene, but the damage had been done. We had lost our advantage. The sheriff was right on our tail, siren wailing.

I looked back and saw Agent Davidson waving like mad for us to pull over. My heart raced. We couldn't get to the river bottoms fast enough. Looking forward, I saw Slate Run Road coming upon us quick. I knew we could head that way, but it was a sharp ninety-degree entrance. Throttle didn't even consider it. He blew by it like it wasn't there. Clearly he had other ideas. Right up the road sat the old run-down middle school building, and right alongside it ran River Road, which would take you all the way down to the river between the cornfields.

I saw right then what Throttle was thinking. He was gonna use the abandoned parking lot of the school building to make a fast and wide swing down River Road. He was going way too fast to make the turn onto River Road directly, but Throttle just let the momentum sling the Charger, drifting and squealing, through the large empty lot until he could steer back into the turn and jump right up on River Road with a head of steam. I don't think he ever let off that accelerator through the whole thing. Now we were screaming toward the river with corn rows whistling by on both sides of the car. I looked back past Ben and Lilly and saw the sheriff's car tearing down the road as well.

"Gonna be awfully hard to shake 'em!" Ben yelled out.

Just then Throttle turned right into the cornfield. "I'm gonna figure-eight 'em!" Throttle yelled.

I had no idea what Throttle was talking about. But there were stalks and ears of corn bouncing everywhere. He seemed to be driving in a large circular pattern. We swooped around in another direction and darted straight ahead. We were mowing down cornstalks at a vicious rate. I turned and looked out the right window and noticed the river was right there. We were racing parallel to the river!

Throttle started to jerk the car away from the river and onto a road, but as soon as we could see where we were going, the sheriff's car appeared from nowhere, headed directly at us. We were going to smash head-on! Throttle violently turned the wheel to the right, narrowly missing the front of the other car.

But a stump concealed in the grass was directly in the path of Throttle's left front tire. Without warning the car made a violent surge upward over the stump, causing the Charger to take flight and barrel-roll toward the river.

I don't know how many times we flipped, but we ended up in the river upside-down. I think I was totally ejected from the car because after I hit the water and got my bearings, I was a good thirty feet from the sinking car. The subsequent events happened in a blur. I was in shock.

I saw Throttle's head emerge from the water. He was screaming, "My leg! I broke my leg!"

The sheriff and Agent Davidson were already swimming for the car. I couldn't see Ben or Lilly. I started swimming for the car too. "Ben!" I yelled, gagging on a mouthful of dirty river water. The car was sinking fast. Sheriff Jenkins dove under and toward the car. I looked up to see Agent Davison pulling Throttle toward the shore as his agonizing screams continued.

I started to dive too, but just as I did, Ben's head surfaced, and he gasped for air. "Lilly!" he screamed. I dove down through the murky water and found a hold on one of the doors of the Charger. I tried to pull myself inside the car, but there was too much confusion—I couldn't see, and I was running out of air. I had to swim back to the top.

When I surfaced, I heard sirens approaching. Davidson was tending to Throttle on the shore. Where was Ben? Where was Lilly? I was starting to fade when the sheriff's large arm swung underneath my shoulders and he started hauling me toward the shore. I was reaching in the direction of the sunken car and being towed in the opposite direction by the sheriff when my vision blurred and I felt consciousness slip away from me.

When I came to, the late-day sun was sinking low in the sky and dimly glaring off the river. I was beside Ben, and deputies Quills and Allen were wrapping a big blanket around us. I look down the bank a ways, and the scene wasn't pretty. Agent Davidson was still tending to a wailing Throttle, and the sheriff was storming toward us, just steps away.

"Either of you two hurt?" he asked.

We both shook our heads no.

"Well, you boys are about to be in a world of it!" he barked as he turned to Deputy Quills. "Take these two up to the jailhouse, lock them up downstairs, and get back here, pronto."

"Yes, sir," Quills said.

22

THE POLICE STATION IN CRIPPLE Creek contained two cells. They were in an out-of-sight, out-of-mind spot, tucked in the back of the municipal building. Positioned between custodial and laundry, the cells didn't see much traffic. Occasionally there was a good ole boy who had gotten a little too liquored up and become rowdy and just needed a place to sleep it off, a place where he couldn't do any damage. Tonight one of the cells housed two people who perhaps had the most serious charges leveled against them in the history of this place.

Ben appeared shaken, on the edge of shock. I didn't know what to say to him. Thankfully, he broke the silence.

"What have we done here, Ed?" he said as he choked back tears.

"It all happened so quick that maybe they'll find her."

Ben stayed silent for a moment, wiping his nose. "Ed," he said, looking up at me and grabbing my arm, "who do you think she is? Really, I mean, c'mon, something's going on here, and we haven't had time to even think about it."

"I know. She seemed to be leading us somewhere, and I think that somewhere is the cellar out behind Harold Stillwater's place," I said as I paced back and forth in the cell.

"I know, but look at us! We're in serious trouble here, man!" Ben was more stressed than a treed raccoon. Our trip to the Stillwater place had been cut a little short. Ben was right. We were in a bad spot.

We heard a door open down the hallway in the direction of the laundry facility. This wouldn't have seemed strange except this building was presently deserted, unless you counted Hot Rod's corpse. Even the agents had left to join in the search down at the river. Upon hearing footsteps, I approached the bars that separated us from freedom. I grasped two of the cold bars and pressed my face between them, trying to look down the hallway.

"Who is it?" Ben whispered from behind me.

The steps continued toward us. I could now see why inmates liked mirrors. When you're locked in a jail cell, it is impossible to see what's coming at you from the sides. It hit me that I was quite possibly on my way to learning other little tidbits about prison life. I cringed for a moment.

As the footsteps neared, I stood back. Ben got up and stood beside me as the approaching figure stepped in front of the cell.

My heart nearly exploded as I laid eyes on the most beautiful creature on earth. There in the dark hallway stood Cristina.

23

T HE RIVER WAS LIT UP like it was high noon. Every fire truck, police cruiser, and boat belonging to Johnson County was present. Besides that, a throng of locals had arrived with their bass boats, johnboats, and such, and people were ranging up and down both sides of the river with flashlights and spotlights. Even Agent Davidson seemed impressed with the effort. Still, the search had yet to produce Lilly. Throttle had been sent by ambulance to a hospital in Lexington; he had a nasty open fracture of his lower leg that needed surgical attention. And once they'd figured out that Ben and I were no worse for the wear, they'd scooted us out of there and to jail in a hurried fashion. A diver had already been sent down to the wreckage to confirm that Lilly was not still trapped inside, so the focus was on the river and the bank. The rescue was frantic from the get-go, but the hopes of finding Lilly alive were ebbing as time passed. It was slowly turning into a recovery mission, although nobody had started calling it that yet.

24

A s Cristina stood there with tears in her eyes, her lip quivered as if she wanted to say something that was too painful to speak of. Ben and I just looked at her for a moment. She dropped her head.

"I'm sorry, Ben. They haven't found anything yet," she said. "The whole town is down there looking for her."

"Cristina, sweetie," I said as I stepped forward to the bars that separated us. I reached one hand through, toward her.

"What's happened here, Eddie?" She sniffled and wiped the tears from her face. "I mean ... first Rodney shoots himself, then Lilly appears outta nowhere looking the same as she did the day she went missing, then you guys take off with her, and now this."

Ben said nothing, but I could hear him sobbing behind me. A tear ran down my face as I stared into Cristina's eyes. I searched for the words, but they didn't come.

She finally reached out and grabbed my hand. I pulled her toward me, and we embraced, as much as you can between bars anyway.

"I don't know, Cris. It's all happened so fast. Ever since last night, we haven't had time to think." I paused. "But there's something else."

"What do you mean?"

"Remember when we were at Ben's house, and we were showing her old diary to her, hoping she would recognize it or something? Well … we ended up taking it with us when we bolted, and I got to looking through it at Throttle's house.

"One of the entries toward the end mentioned Lilly having trouble with a guy up at the Jamboree, and get this, she says to me, 'Stillwater.' So I figured it was Hot Rod, but when I asked her about it, she said it was his pa, Old Man Stillwater.

"And that's not all. Every time we mentioned something about Lilly, she would talk like we weren't even talking about her. She would refer to herself as 'her' or 'she.' Throttle said she was talking in the third person, or something. I don't know, but it was *spooky*.

"There's something about the Stillwater place, especially out in their cellar, that Lilly was talking about. The whole thing is way out there, I know, but we were thinking we should go up there and have a look around … that is, until we crashed into the river.

"Your pa, you know how he feels about me anyway. He was so angry! He wouldn't even let me speak. And with the frantic search going on down there and all, he had Ben and me rushed right over here and thrown into the pokey. Throttle is in bad shape. His leg was busted up real good." I took a deep breath after finishing.

"I know, Ed. I had a funny feeling about this thing the whole time, especially ever since I saw Lilly," said Cristina. She was looking at me with those faraway eyes that indicated something was becoming clear in her head.

"Me too," Ben finally said. "I really wanted it to be her, I did. But I saw the way she and my pa looked at each other. Something about it really shook him, and he's an oak."

Cristina stepped back and put her hand to her mouth like she was contemplating something real hard.

"What is it?" I asked. I knew her well, and I knew that look.

"I know I shouldn't do this." She turned and began walking away.

"Do what? Cristina!" I shouted after her.

"I'll be right back," she mumbled. She sounded like she had the weight of the world on her.

***

She returned with Mexican Joe after about fifteen minutes had passed. Ole Joe had been a part of the community since before I was born, and he was the only Latino in Johnson County. When he was a child, he was adopted by the Jameses, who had their farm out by the elementary school. Years before Lilly's disappearance and reappearance, Homer James was working for an outfit that was drilling for oil down in Texas, and there he became friends with Joe's dad. In a tragic accident Joe's dad was killed, and somehow, when things were all settled, and because there was no señora, Homer ended up with Joe. So when he came back home here to Cripple Creek from the oilfields, he had a five-year-old Mexican boy in tow. They raised him as their own, and he just became part of the hill folk. His real name was José, but somewhere along the line, someone said, "José—that's Mexican for Joe," and it stuck. Thus, Mexican Joe.

"Joe, how's it going?" Ben said. I was glad to see Joe. He was good people. If you ever needed help, he was always there.

"Fair to middlin'," Joe said with a smile. Joe spoke like everyone else 'cause he'd been raised around a bunch of hillbillies, and I'd bet he couldn't speak a lick of Spanish.

"Joe's gonna run you boys up close to the Stillwater place and drop you off. I can't do it. My dad's expecting me back down at the river, and if I'm away awhile, he'll start suspectin' something. He already suspects that I didn't just volunteer to run up here to fetch a couple extra lights for no reason whatsoever, and ..."

"Cristina, we're still locked in here!" I said, motioning around with my hands at the walls and bars surrounding us.

Cristina held up a few keys on an old ring and jingled them a bit. "You think I'm the sheriff's daughter and I don't know a few little secrets about this place? Daddy has always kept extra keys that he felt were important stashed at home."

"Atta girl!" Ben shouted.

"Cris, you'll be in so much trouble for this."

Cristina fumbled with the keys and inserted the correct one. She looked up at me before turning it in the lock. "There's already too much trouble for this, Eddie, but only you guys were *with her*. Now go an' finish it." She turned the lock and swung the door open.

Within seconds, Ben was already halfway up the hall with Mexican Joe. He turned to see Cristina and me still standing together outside the cell. "C'mon, Ed!" he exclaimed.

"Edison Bestwell," Cristina said softly as she grabbed both sides of my face in her small hands. "I love you—you know I always have. Finish this and get back here safe before we're all found out."

"I love you too, Cris." I leaned down and kissed her quivering lips. I stepped away from her and made my way up the hall to Joe and Ben. Turning back, I said, "Keep your dad distracted as long as you can." I held her stare until the growing distance and darkness of the cell block engulfed us, and we headed up the stairway to the main floor of the municipal building. Mexican Joe revved his engine as we burst through the back door of the building. "You two lay flat in the back until we get outta sight. Stay scarce until we're outta town. When we get near the Stillwater place, I'll slow down, and you boys just roll out without me stoppin', and I'll just keep going down the road like nobody's business."

"Okay, Joe," I said as Ben and I hopped up in the back of his old Ford and lay flat. I heard Cristina's big Chevy 4x4 fire up and head in the opposite direction toward the river bottoms.

It struck me that Cristina must have been thinking about this since the moment her dad threw us in jail. She obviously had filled Mexican Joe in on things. That she'd even thought of Joe was genius. If there was anybody who was in a constant state of lying low, it was him. Oh, how I loved that girl!

25

THE SHERIFF SAW CRISTINA SLOW her big truck as it reached his cruiser. She leaned her head out of the side and yelled, "Pa! Pa! Where you want these here lights?"

"Over there!" he shouted, pointing toward a spot downstream that looked like it could use a little light and a little direction. Deputy Jimmy Allen, a couple of agents, and a few half-drunk locals were trying to concert a focused effort. *Too many chiefs and not enough Indians*, the sheriff thought.

Cristina slammed the big truck in reverse, hit the gas, and swung the front end of the Chevy toward them. The truck rumbled through the high grass and over a few dead trees near the river.

"Here!" Cristina shouted as she handed one of the shockingly bright lights to one of the agents, who focused it along the bank. She quickly grabbed the other one and gave it to Jimmy Allen, if for nothing else than to keep his feelings from getting hurt. "And keep it focused farther out and down the river a ways so we don't miss nothin' coming through this way!" she said.

The sheriff was watching from a ways off, and he was right proud of how she was handling the situation. For a seventeen-year-old, she was handling herself just fine. For a moment he forgot about us boys down at the jail and the events that had led to all of this. He just proudly watched his daughter. But the contentment of the moment didn't linger. He shook his head a bit and remembered how frustrated he was with the bunch of us. Deep down he was rather fond of Ben and me, but we were the ones who had gotten these shenanigans started by bringing Lilly up out of the woods the night before, and he had plenty of questions still unanswered.

Just then Agent Tucker Davidson approached the sheriff. "Harlen, something about this doesn't smell right to me. We pulled them three boys outta there before they could get their undies wet, and yet we can't produce a single shred of evidence of that girl even being in that car with them!" Tucker Davidson turned and slammed his fist down on the top of Sheriff Jenkins's cruiser. "I wanna go talk to them boys right now, Harlen! We've got enough people down here to find Jimmy Hoffa. So how about you and me take a trip up to your jail and get to the bottom of this?"

The sheriff looked at Tucker's hand, which was still resting on the hood of his car. Agent Davidson removed his hand but continued staring at Harlen. The men shared a tense silence. *He's right*, the sheriff thought. *We do need to get to the bottom of this.*

"Good enough, Tucker. We'll do that ... and I got a few questions of my own."

They walked to the sheriff's cruiser, slid in, and headed toward town.

***

Cristina watched her dad and Agent Davidson exchange heated words. For all the commotion going on around her, she couldn't hear what they were saying, but she had a good guess. When they jumped in the sheriff's car and started away, her heart sank. She thought of the empty jail cell in the municipal building. Panic rose up in her.

She turned and looked back at the scene by the river and saw Jimmy watching the sheriff pull away as well. "Jimmy!

Shine your light down that way!" she yelled, pointing out into the river.

As soon as the deputy's attention was diverted back to the river, Cristina turned and ran for her truck. *Think! Think!* she thought to herself.

She jumped up into the still-running truck and forcefully dropped it into gear. All she knew was that she needed to arrive back at the jail before her dad and Agent Davidson. Perhaps she could divert their attention before it was too late, but that was a long shot.

She knew the only way she could arrive before them was to drive through the bottoms and up the steep dirt path that led to the back side of town. So the big blue 4x4 lumbered down the narrow dirt road and around the bend that led to the steep embankment. Cristina's light frame tossed to and fro behind the wheel. She let off the accelerator and slowed ever so briefly as the steep path came into view. Many a local rowdy had successfully climbed the hill in a 4x4, but Cristina had never attempted it. Her anxiety rose another level.

She quickly dismissed the idea of backing off and giving up, knowing the moment required bold measures. She hit the gas again and gripped the steering wheel tight as the truck tore up the hill.

The truck cleared the top of the path with more than enough speed. Cristina let out a shriek as her vehicle launched off the top lip and landed with a thunderous bounce onto Second Street.

She sped the truck down two blocks, turned onto Main Street, and approached the municipal building. With a jerk she stopped aside the empty street and turned off the rumbling motor. In an instant she collapsed on the steering wheel and burst into tears.

26

BEN AND I STAYED FLAT to the bed of Joe's old '59 pickup as it rolled through town. Most everyone was down at the river anyway, but we had to be careful just in case. The Stillwater place, which sat toward the end of Crawford Road, was a few miles out of town and out in the middle of nowhere, but then again, everywhere around Cripple Creek was in the middle of nowhere. The road dead-ended right up past the Stillwater place, so the plan was for Joe to take us just so far, and we'd be on our own from there. It was best to be as quiet and stealthy as we could anyway. Old Man Stillwater brewed shine up around his place and didn't take kindly to folks prowlin' around, and he'd likely be extra jumpy with everything that had recently taken place.

"Ed, what's the plan once we get close?" Ben asked.

"I'm not sure, man. I haven't had a plan since sometime yesterday," I said with half a grin. Ben let out a snort, and we both laughed for a moment.

Pretty soon we felt the road turn from pavement to gravel and knew we were headed out of town.

"All clear, boys," Joe hollered through the sliding window in his cab.

Ben and I sat up in the bed of the pickup and were greeted by the chilly autumn air that swirled around us. Joe was making like everything was normal, just easing out of town like he would on any given night. We both rose to one knee and looked over the roof of the truck as it moved down the road. For a minute we just sat and felt the wind push against us and pull back our hair. *What a pleasant night,* I thought for a moment.

We traveled along the county road a ways, and then Joe slowed his truck as he turned onto Crawford Road. He turned off the headlights of the truck to navigate by moonlight. Ole Joe looked back at us to see if we were payin' attention. We were. I nodded at Joe, and so did Ben.

"Up here a ways I'm gonna let you fellers out," Joe said in his hillbilly accent. I always thought it novel how a Mexican had ended up with such a way of speech. "In a minute I'm gonna start slowing down. When you boys feel comfortable with it, jump out the back of the truck and keep on a runnin' till you can bring yourselves to a stop. Best if I don't have to hit the brakes 'cause of the lights and all, ya know, Eddie."

"Sounds good to me, Joe," I said. "And listen, thanks for this, okay?"

"Glad to help out," Joe said as he returned his attention to the road. Then he turned back again, reached through the back window, and put his hand on my arm. "You boys *really found her?*"

Ben and I looked at each other for a moment. I looked back at Joe. "Yeah, we did."

With that, Ben and I scooted to the back of the bed of the truck. We climbed over the back and stood on the bumper as we held on to the tailgate. Mexican Joe slowed a bit more, and Ben and I jumped down to the road. Our legs floundered about as we battled the laws of physics, but we soon came to a stop without incident. We watched the shadow of the truck meander up the road and disappear around the bend.

***

Ben and I slithered through the woods toward the Stillwater place with great caution. It was now dark all around. The canopy of trees resisted any intrusion of starlight. I could feel my heart beating in my chest and hear it in my ears. All instinct and common sense told me to get out, go back into town, back to the hoosegow, and tell the sheriff everything we knew. Let the cavalry take care of it. But I was compelled by some unseen force to continue on.

We topped out over a little rise in the forest floor and saw the first hints of light coming from the Stillwater house. We laid down at the top of the rise, the autumn leaves crumpling under our weight.

Ben took a deep breath. "That's it, isn't it?"

"Yep," I said.

It had been a long time since either of us had been to Rodney's place. There wasn't exactly an inviting spirit to the place, ya know. The two-bedroom shanty sat in a small clearing that was dominated by Old Man Stillwater's rummage. Two broken-down cars that would never run again, an old Coke machine, a washing machine, a dog house, and three picnic tables cluttered with implements and car parts littered the backyard. And somewhere, tucked away in a small, dark corner of the woods, sat the moonshine still, a place you didn't want to get caught prowlin' around. And then there was the cellar, which would be easy to miss. The low-profile, old wooden doors were the same color as the surrounding earth and leaves.

We spent the next half hour creeping closer toward the dim light of the back porch. The soft glow cast ominous shadows from the junk scattered about the yard. The old codger's truck sat out front, and there were lights on in the house, but we'd yet to see him. That made me nervous as a cat. Was he lurking about, watching us?

Soon we were within twenty feet of the cellar. The plan wasn't a complex one—go in and snoop around. There was something about that cellar; I could feel it.

"What if it's locked?" Ben asked.

"Don't jinx us."

"No, really, Ed. What if it is? And what if we do get in? Then what?"

"Shh," I said. "Stop it! Let's just go and see."

27

THE TRIP TOWARD TOWN TO the municipal building started off as cold as anyone probably would've expected. Neither the sheriff nor Agent Davidson said much. Deep down on some level, I think they had some mutual, if only professional, respect for each other. They had been thrown back into this situation that had brought them together seven years ago, and they wanted the same outcome: to find Lilly and tie up the loose ends that had haunted both of them for the better part of the last decade. Finally, the sheriff broke the ice.

"Whatcha been doing with yourself all these years, Tucker?"

"Quite honestly, Harlen, I've been trying to forget about this place and move on with my career, which hasn't been that easy. Every missing person case I have worked on has reminded me somehow of this one. How about you, Sheriff?"

"Kinda the same. It's hard to get away from it in such a small town. When I actually laid eyes on that girl yesterday, it just seemed so surreal. I'm telling you, Tucker, as sure as I'm sitting here, that girl looked the exact same as I remember her ... but there was something way off about her too."

"I'm listening."

"I can't really put my finger on it, but when I talked with her dad, Earl Baldridge, he said something about her eyes and it not being his girl, and Earl Baldridge doesn't say *anything* unless he means it."

"I kinda gathered that. And what about those boys? They don't seem like criminals, and the one is Lilly's brother, right?"

"Yeah, good kids, never been in any trouble. I think you spooked 'em, pulling up here with your posse. I think they thought that you were gonna take off with her, and I'm not so sure I totally disagree with 'em." The sheriff shot the agent a serious stare. Agent Davidson looked back at him but did not answer.

They were pulling around the corner from River Street onto Main Street, just a block from the municipal building, when they saw Cristina Jenkins's large 4x4 truck blocking the parking place where the sheriff usually parked. Cristina was standing outside the truck on the driver's side, with her hands tucked deep down into the pockets of her jeans and her head bowed low. Sheriff Jenkins knew his daughter well, and this body language meant she had done something bad, something that would disappoint her daddy.

"What's this all about?" Agent Davidson asked.

The sheriff said nothing as he pulled up beside her truck and shut off his engine. When the sheriff and the agent approached Cristina, she raised her head to look at them, tears streaming down her face.

"I'm sorry, Daddy, but ..." she sobbed.

"Sorry for what?" Davidson coldly interjected.

The sheriff held up a hand toward the agent and just walked around her and into the municipal building. Tucker Davidson followed close behind, not saying a word. They marched quickly through the hallway that led to the back of the building and descended the steps. As they neared the end of the hallway that housed the jail cells and Harlen saw that they were empty, his heart sank.

The sheriff angrily kicked the open door of the jail cell, and it slammed closed with a mighty clang. "Daggummit!" he exclaimed loud enough to be heard all the way outside. He could hear his daughter sobbing harder out in the parking lot.

28

BEN AND I FELT COMFORTABLE enough to creep within feet of the cellar entrance. To my delight, it looked as if there was no lock on the latch that fastened the two doors.

"Easy," I whispered as Ben reached down to pull on one of the old latches. The door groaned against the force of gravity, and I stepped up to give him a hand. We managed to pull one door completely up and lay it back against the earth. The cellar emitted a stale and sickening odor. For a minute we just stood there and peered down into the darkness. We could make out a couple of the top steps that led down into the pit. Most people used their cellars as a hideout for tornados and for food stores, but I had a feeling that there was more than just canned beans and jugs of water and moonshine down there. The look on Ben's face said he felt the same way.

As we were looking into the abyss, the sound of a shell being pumped into the chamber of a shotgun came from behind us. My heart stopped and rose into my throat as I heard Old Man Stillwater say, "Finding anything interestin', boys?"

We instinctively raised our arms above our heads. My heart had restarted, and it felt like it was trying to escape from my chest with every beat. I knew Ben had to feel the same way. As I tried to gather my thoughts, I heard a sickening thud and saw Ben's head lurch forward as he stumbled toward the black abyss of the cellar. I quickly turned my head to face our assailant, but as I did, I felt the impact of the butt of the shotgun on the side of my head. I saw stars as I fell forward into the darkness.

***

I found myself standing in the corner of the cellar. The last thing I remembered was feeling a couple of dull impacts throughout my body as I fell. The wind roared outside, and the walls shook. The cellar doors were shut, and the hinges were creaking. The two heavy wooden doors seemed to breathe with the storm as the atmospheric pressure changed by the moment deep in the cellar. At one moment they would heave upward, ready to burst open, and then the doors would sink onto the jambs as if a great weight had been set upon them. I heard things blowing by and tumbling above me as the storm's crescendo intensified—a bicycle, a swing set, a large oak perhaps. This unnerved me because the weather had been quite pleasant the last time I stood up there on terra firma, and this was all-around different. I was frozen in a dark corner of the cellar, with the only light coming from the great flashes of lightning bursting through the cracks in the doors. I tried to move, but it was impossible; I was in a dreamlike state, the kind that won't let you move from the railroad tracks as the train approaches.

I heard voices outside, or was it the wind? Then came the creaking of the latch. Light, wind, and debris raced down the steps as one of the cellar doors burst open. Then the voices became screams and curses as feet appeared at the top of the steps. Harold Stillwater descended the stairs, dragging Lilly by a handful of hair. A gust of wind caught the other cellar door, which nearly came unhinged as it flew open as well. I tried to yell something and move toward Stillwater and Lilly, but I felt myself restrained by the paralyzing force that had overtaken me. When he reached the bottom of the steps, Stillwater dragged Lilly to the back of the cellar. Her screams were terrible.

"Shut up!" he yelled as he backhanded her across the face.

Lilly's protests abated as the forceful blow stunned her. Blood ran from her mouth and nose. I screamed at Harold Stillwater, but my voice was muted by the same force that was denying my efforts to move. In some recess of my mind, I knew I was witnessing events of the past. The energy from these past events was so strong that my subconscious was able to cross the barrier between present reality and past reality. Lightning flashed and thunder roared as Harold's eyes gleamed with a perverse delight. He reached down and grabbed her shirt and ripped it from her body.

"No!" Lilly screamed. She tried to get up, but her attacker threw his weight on her, pinning her to the cellar floor.

"Please, God, no!" she cried out as Harold reached down and clawed at Lilly's shorts. He was winning the fight. He put his forearm across her chest and raised his torso off her so that his free hand could go about the business of undoing his own pants.

His arm was choking her, suffocating her, and all of a sudden, she gave up fighting. She rolled her eyes upward, away from her assailer, and coughed out barely audible words: "I forgive you." Harold Stillwater froze. He looked at her in horror as if his previously inert humanity was slowly coming to life. The storm raged outside, and a great bolt of lightning struck somewhere close. In an instant the cellar lit up like noonday, and a tremendous thunderclap shook the floor. In that instant Harold beheld the pure terror on Lilly's bloodied face. He stared down into her frightened eyes.

"I forgive you," she whispered again.

Harold seemed suddenly frozen. In an instant he rolled from her and lay flat on his back. Terrified, Lilly sprang up and darted for the steps leading out of the cellar. When she was nearly to the top and on her way to freedom, a mighty gust caught the open door and brought it slamming shut, catching Lilly full force on her head and sending her tumbling down the stairs. She lay motionless at the bottom, just feet from Stillwater.

Harold scrambled over to where she lay and brushed the bloody hair away from her face. Her eyes were wide and lifeless. He laid his head against her chest to listen for a heartbeat, but apparently, there was none. "No ... no!" he shouted. A tear ran down Harold Stillwater's anguished face. "I was letting you go," he said, sobbing.

At that instant, Rodney came rushing down the cellar stairs in a panic. "Pa, there's a tornado that's been spotted just ..." He froze when he saw the scene before him. He started to back up the steps. "Is that Lilly Bald ...?"

"Shut up, boy, and get down here!"

Rodney slowly descended the stairs. His mouth gaped in shock as his eyes moved from his father to Lilly's lifeless body.

"Get over here, boy, and help me bury this body!" Harold was already up and fetching a couple of shovels from the back of the cellar.

"Wha ..."

"Shut your mouth and start diggin', boy!" Harold screamed as he thrust a shovel into Rodney's hand.

With a terrified look on his face, Rodney began to help his father dig in the earthen floor of the cellar. I felt my contact with this past reality starting to fade. The vision of it blurred as I sensed myself being drawn back through a sort of tunnel of darkness and mist, as if by some gravitational force that was beyond my control. Soon all became black and nothingness.

***

When I came to, I found myself bound to a pole that sat nearly in the middle of the cellar floor. The light was low, and my vision was blurry. I knew that Ben was tied up with me, on the other side of the pole, because I could feel his fingers and hands struggling against the cord that dug into the skin of our wrists. The memory of what I'd just seen was still clear in my head. *Was that a dream?* I thought. I turned my head sharply to the left to see if I could get a glimpse of Ben, and a bolt of pain shot from a lump on the back of my head all the way to the soles of my feet. I let out a groan.

"You with me, Ed?" I heard Ben say.

"Yeah, I think so. My ..."

"Shut your pie holes, the both of ya!" Old Man Stillwater barked as he stepped into view from a dark recess of the room. He still held the shotgun. "Just what do you fellers think you're doing, prowling around where you shouldn't be?"

"I know it was you! You brought her down here!" I snapped back at the old codger, not knowing where my courage was coming from.

Harold Stillwater looked at me with what seemed to be bewilderment and a touch of insanity. Behind me Ben mumbled, "What?"

"You best shut your mouth, boy!"

It was then that I caught the faint sound of a siren. I didn't know whether the old man heard it right off, but a surge of courage and confidence came over me. I suddenly realized exactly why Rodney had shot himself.

"You buried her down here, and you made your boy help you!" I looked over toward the spot where they had been digging in my dream or vision or whatever it was that I had just experienced. "Over there!" I added for good measure.

The siren became louder, and Mr. Stillwater tilted his ear up. I saw fear in his eyes. I figured that Cristina had sooner or later been forced to tell her daddy everything, and they now were quickly approaching the Stillwater compound. Harold looked at us with increasing panic.

"Give yourself up!" Ben blurted out.

"I didn't kill her," the old man said as he slumped to his knees.

"I know," I said.

"What?" Ben shouted.

I heard the sounds of footsteps, and red and blue light began to filter in through the cracks in the cellar doors. Someone grabbed one of the doors and tried lifting it, but it was latched from the inside.

"Help, we're down here!" Ben yelled.

Something heavy slammed against the cellar door—they were trying to break in. I looked back to Harold Stillwater, and what I saw horrified me. He had set the butt of the shotgun on the ground and had the barrel placed under his chin. Another loud crack came from above us as the old cellar door began to splinter. Harold reached down toward the trigger.

"Nooo!" I screamed. My voice was drowned out by the roar of the shotgun blast.

29

SURE ENOUGH, THEY FOUND REMAINS buried in the cellar. The bones were identified as that of an adolescent female. That part was clear enough. What they couldn't do, however, was determine that it was in fact Lilly. It would've been case closed if it hadn't been for the fact that over the past day about a dozen people had seen her walking around, breathing air, as big as you please.

The best way to match a skeleton to a missing person in 1986 was to use dental records to match up the teeth in the skull with the teeth of the deceased. But the problem was, Lilly had never seen a dentist. Nell said she never complained of a toothache all her life. Imagine that.

After a short discussion between the sheriff and Agent Davidson, it was decided that no charges would be filed against me or Ben. That just would've complicated matters anyway. Tucker Davidson could now close the only case that had remained unsolved in his otherwise illustrious career. The last time I saw him was down at the municipal building when he was getting ready to leave town. He shook my hand, looked at me with a furrowed brow, and said, "I guess I'll never be hearing from you boys again."

"Guess not," I replied, and we looked at each other with that "I know that you know that I know" kinda look. And with that he left our lives forever.

Mexican Joe never let on like he'd heard or seen a thing.

The three of us were not about to give him up as the one who'd given us a ride out there. Besides, the sheriff never really dug too hard anyway. The brouhaha down at the river really died down when the people found out what was happening out at the Stillwater place. Besides, they weren't finding anything down there anyway. There was a memorial service for Lilly once the remains were found. The whole town attended, and most folks found their closure there in some form or fashion.

Now, who did we find that night in the barn? Will Ben and I ever know? Perhaps we have to begin to think the way children do. Like I said before, the closer you are to infancy, the closer you are to the way things really work in the ether—that place where your soul comes into this world, the same place your soul crosses after you give up the ghost. Things don't work here the way they work there, ya know. That's just the way it is. And through the ages the stories go.

That's the way small towns are down here in the hills of Kentucky—what can't be explained becomes lore. The stories of those few days will ebb and flow like the fog that settles in the hollows early in the cool morning. Heck, I guess every place has its own little stories, ya know. They'll surely be talked about 'round many a campfire fantastical in the fog of physics and moonshine. But the light of day will come and burn off the fog, leaving only what was there to begin with. I know what happened that night. I was there. Just like the Indians knew more than we give 'em credit for. When Tecumseh was born, his father, Pucksinwah, raised his eyes to the sky to give thanks to the Great Spirit for the birth of the child. And when he did, a large meteor tore through the atmosphere, the grand ether, and he named his son the Panther Passing Across—Tecumseh. The Indians who roamed these hills before us had their stories. And I reckon we do too.